The Cannibals

THE CURSE OF THE JOLLY STONE TRILOGY—BOOK II

IAIN LAWRENCE

LAUREL-LEAF BOOKS

Published by Laurel-Leaf
an imprint of Random House Children's Books
a division of Random House, Inc.
New York

Originally published in hardcover in the United States by
Delacorte Press, New York, in 2005. This edition published by
arrangement with Delacorte Press.

www.randomhouse.com/teens

Educators and librarians, for a variety of teaching tools,
visit us at www.randomhouse.com/teachers

RL: 5.6
ISBN: 978-0-440-41933-4
First Laurel-Leaf Edition
June 2007
Printed in the United States of America
10 9 8 7 6 5 4 3 2 1

for my big brother,
Hamish,
and his family:
Danielle, Andrew, Iain, and Lisa

I wish you all were nearer.

contents

one
BEYOND THE CAPE OF STORMS

I came to know my father as we voyaged to Australia. At first he seemed a different man, his face sunburnt and bright, wrinkled round the eyes into a never-ending smile. Gone was his weariness, and years from his age. But he hadn't really changed; I had only forgotten. Along with his sea clothes, he had donned his old self, becoming again the man I had known as a child.

I grew to love him as I had then, and saw my love returned, though not the way I wanted. Father could see that my time in the prison hulk had left me pale and thin, but not that I was stronger on the inside because of it. So he vowed to keep me safe, and cared so deeply for me that it proved our undoing in the end.

Five months out of England, we rounded the Cape of

Good Hope. We *stormed* around it, in furious winds and tumbling cliffs of water. But I saw nothing but a patch of sky, a glimpse of sails through the ragged holes in an old tarpaulin.

A tangled fate had made my father my jailer, and now he was sailing me beyond the seas, in a ship that had been a slaver. He was the captain and I was a convict.

With sixty others I was penned below, in the dark and shuddering hull of the ship. The wind howled and tore at the tarpaulin that covered the hatch. Whole waves exploded through the grating, and for every drop of water that rained through the deck seams, a bucket's load welled up through the timbers.

I found that I had not beaten my old fear of the sea. For nine days running I lay sick as a dog on my wooden berth, almost wishing for the ship to founder, yet terrified that it might. I clung to the ringbolts where the slaves had been chained, listening to the ocean batter at the planks. If it weren't for Midgely I might have gone as mad as my poor mother. He was young and small, blinded in both eyes. But he stayed at my side, little Midge.

When the Cape was behind us, the weather cleared. The hatches were opened, and up we went to a sunlit morning.

My father was too kindhearted to be a jailer. Perhaps his spell in debtors' prison had taught him the misery of confinement. He always gave us the run of the deck on fair-weather days. He'd let the crew indulge us with seafaring stories, and from time to time he had the fiddler play while we danced. Our prison wasn't the ship, but the sea itself.

On this day we milled like cattle in the small space between the masts. Sailors were tightening the lashings on the piles of planks and timbers. Others worked high in the rigging, but it made me dizzy to turn up my head to watch them. Every sail was set, the brig pushing along below its towers of canvas. The air was hot. Water steamed from the deck and the sails and the rigging.

A sailor came for Midge and me. We were hurried off, up to the afterdeck and down to the cabins. My father was waiting below, standing by his broad windows that looked back where the ship had been. Our silvery wake stretched over the waves like the trail of a slug.

"Good morning, Captain Tin," cried Midgely.

Father turned to greet us, a great smile on his face. "Good morning, William," he said. He was the only one to call Midgely by his proper name. His hand fell upon my shoulder. "Are you bearing up, Tom?" he asked.

I nodded.

"You've weathered the storm, I see."

"Oh, yes, sir," said Midge. "It was a ripping storm, weren't it?"

Father smiled. "Sit, boys," he said, waving us toward his berth.

I took Midgely's hand to guide him to our place. He could hardly see at all, and never when he went from sunshine into shadows. But he pulled away, and went straight to my father's berth, dodging the table and dodging the chair. He'd learned the cabin well in the dozen visits we'd made. When I climbed beside him on the bed, it seemed the height of luxury to sit on a mattress again.

"What would you like?" asked Father. "Cheese? Bread and jam?" He always offered, and we always refused.

3

I went straight to the point. "Father, we have a plan," I said.

He stood with his hands behind his back. The sea tilted and slashed across his windows, and he leaned from side to side against the roll of the ship. The motions made my stomach churn.

"We want to escape," I said.

Father looked surprised. His mouth, for a moment, gaped open. Then a hearty laugh came out. "Escape?" he asked. His hand motioned toward the huge sea. "To where?"

Midgely answered. "To a place near Tetakari Island, sir."

"Where the devil's that?"

"South and east of Borneo," said Midge. "But not as far as Java."

My father frowned. He crossed the cabin to his table, then reached up to the rafters. His charts were stowed there, rolled into tubes, and he talked as he sorted through them. "I've never heard of such a place," he said.

"Well, there's an island near it what looks like an elephant," said Midge. "The cliffs and the trees, they look like the elephant's head. There's a sandy beach, and coconuts and breadfruit. It was in the book. Ask Tom, sir. Ask him if it ain't true."

Father picked through his charts. "Well, books are travelers' tales, you know. The writers fill them with nonsense."

"But this one was wrote by a reverend, sir," said Midge.

My father smiled back at him. Like every sailor on the brig, he adored little Midge. My friend might have been the ship's cat for all the pats and treats that came his way. "Let's have a look at your elephant island," he said.

4

He pulled out a chart and unrolled it, placing little weights on the corners, then leaned down with his hands on the table edge.

I stood beside him. I had never found my sea legs, and the ship tried to pitch me around like a skittle. It tossed me away from the table, then pushed me against it. My head spinning, I stared at the chart.

There were hundreds of islands drawn there, and most looked as small as peppercorns. At once, our plan seemed foolish. I couldn't count the hours we'd spent in the pages of Midgely's book, traveling from island to island with the reverend writer. Midgely, especially, had escaped from our prison ship into the book. In a fashion, he had taken me with him, out of the hulk and in through the etchings and the printed words, into the islands of the South Seas. When he had been blinded—when that dreadful Benjamin Penny had punctured his eyes—Midge had relied on me to read him the tales, and to tell him the pictures. I'd thought I could glance at any chart and pick out all the places we had read about.

But now it seemed hopeless. How could we ever find our way among those hundreds of islands when I couldn't tell one from another?

"Here's Borneo," said Father, reaching down to the chart. His fingers touched a large island, then slid across the paper. "Here's Java. So if your book is right—and I don't believe for a moment that it is—your island would be somewhere here." His hand moved in a spiral over the scattering of islands. "Well, as you can see . . ." He leaned closer to the table. "By George!" he breathed. "There it is. Tetakari."

"See? I *knew* it was true," cried Midgely. "Tom and me, we can sail to there. If you let us off in a boat, we can sail from island to island."

Father looked up. He didn't turn toward Midge on the berth, but stared straight at me. "That's your plan?" he asked. "*That's* your scheme?"

"Yes, sir," I said, as boldly as I could.

"Well, it's foolish." He shook his head. "I won't be a party to it."

"But, Father, we have to escape," I told him. "It's all lost if we get to Australia. They'll put us in chains and we'll never get home again."

"Oh, you'll not *stay* in Australia," said he. "You may lay to that, Tom. Don't think I haven't been dwelling on this myself."

The ship lurched over the crest of a wave. A shadow flitted across the table, and I looked up at the windows to see an albatross gliding across the glass.

"I shall take you to Australia," said Father. "But I shan't put you ashore. I'll say straight out that Mr. Goodfellow plotted against us, that's he's hounded us for years. I'll call for the governor, or whoever's in charge, and tell him the whole story."

"But he won't believe a word," I said.

"Come, come," said Father. "It's a tangled tale, I'll grant you that, but tell it we must. Have we any choice?"

"Do we *ever* have a choice?" I asked, which made him frown in puzzlement.

I had learned that the lives of men and women were decided only by chance. We were as twigs in a stream, unable to choose our course, knocked hither and yon by the currents and eddies of fate. For most of my life, luck had been with me. By chance I'd been born with a twin, joined together—flesh and blood—by a bit of skin so small that my father had easily cut us apart. Through no choice of mine, we were born in a tempest, so that fate gave me an everlasting fear of the sea. But the same fate saw my father take hold of me while my twin was snatched away by the storm. So I had gone off to school to become a gentleman, while my twin, saved from the storm by a fisherman, grew up as a vagrant in the streets of London. He became known as the Smasher, one of the gang of urchins ruled by the Darkey, a mysterious woman whose own river of fate had since carried her off to the gallows.

It had seemed the luckiest day of my life when fate led me to the banks of the Thames, to unearth the most fabulous diamond in all the world. Only later did I wonder if it wasn't the Jolly Stone, that famous jewel with a terrible curse. Right then I had felt on top of the world, though—in truth—I was really balanced on the edge of a great cataract in my river of destiny.

I tumbled down it that day, and into a raging whirlpool. And, ever since, I'd been trapped in that current. There the lives of myself and my twin joined together again. I met old Worms, the body snatcher, who took me to my twin's very grave, down to the earth where his moldering body lay, and when I rose again I was him. Round and round I went in that whirlpool. My diamond was left in the empty grave, while I was delivered to the hands of the Darkey, and to those who had known the Smasher, to Benjamin Penny and Gaskin

Boggis, and on to Weedle himself, whom the Smasher had disfigured so cruelly.

So I knew there was no gain in battling chance. But I had learned something else as well: that a man could become so rich and powerful that he could change the course of fate's long river. Such a man was Mr. Goodfellow, he who had hounded my father into debtors' prison, then tricked him into sailing his filthy ships.

How his eyes had glowed with greed when he heard of my diamond! He offered a bargain: my life for that stone. But I wanted its riches and wouldn't give them up. So I kept the secret, and it was Mr. Goodfellow—not fate—that sent me to Australia.

Now only the diamond could set me free. I had to unearth that stone from its churchyard grave, then use its powers to set Mr. Goodfellow adrift in the terrible river. But I had to get home to do that, or neither myself nor my father would ever be free.

two

WE PLAN OUR ESCAPE

Not all of the crew could be trusted. There was one man aboard the brig who watched our every move, who did double duty, we were sure, serving the owner, the wretched Mr. Goodfellow. In turns, my father suspected the bosun, the mate, and the cook, but I'd cast in my teeth with the steward. The fellow had ears as big as blinkers, and a habit of lurking close to the great cabin whenever I was there.

On this day, as we bowled through the seas below the great Cape, his shadow lay on the deck, head and shoulders in the doorway. Father and Midgely and I did our scheming in whispers. Midgely had moved from the berth, and all three of us stood braced against the table, where the spread-open chart fluttered and shifted with each roll of the ship.

"I don't care for this plan of yours," said Father. "Do you

really think I can turn you loose in a boat and send you off through the islands?"

The ocean tilted in his big stern windows. The ship rattled and groaned as it climbed the swells.

"We won't get lost," said Midgely. "We know the book."

"That isn't what I meant," said Father. "It's the 'how,' William." He cupped his hands, as though the word were a thing he could hold. "The *how*. If it's seen that I'm helping convicts escape, we'll all be put in chains as soon as we reach Australia."

"We've thought of that," said I.

Midgely nodded. "We know we're on our own hook, sir."

How my father smiled at that sailor's expression! I said, "No one will know you've helped us. We'll launch the longboat ourselves and . . ."

Father looked astonished. "The longboat? You're just going to shove it over the side, are you? Just push it off and hop in?" He scratched his head. "Do you know how much the longboat weighs?"

"How much, sir?" asked Midge.

Father's breath exploded; his hands flew out. "I don't know," said he. "It takes four men with blocks and tackles to hoist it up and over. That's how much it weighs."

"But ain't it worth a go?" asked Midge.

The ship stumbled through a trough. The masts shook and the rudder creaked, and there came a rattle from the doorway. The steward stepped in, carrying a tray. "Tea and biscuits, Captain Tin," he said. "Will the young *convicts* be joining you, sir?"

"No," said Father, as the man well knew. Midge and I

never ate in the cabin; we didn't want to be noseys. "Leave it and go," said he.

The steward carried his tray to the smaller table, the one that hung in gimbals. He had to pass beside me, tipping the tray to keep it level. I didn't watch him put it down. I had been sickened before by the sight of that table sitting still in its gimbals as the cabin reeled and rocked.

"Studying the islands again are you, sir?" asked the steward. "Teaching the young convicts geography, sir?"

"That will be all, Bede," said Father.

"You might better teach them the fear of God, if I may say so."

"You may not."

"It's what they'll need in Australia, sir. A good, smacking fear of God. And a fear of the lash, of course."

"I said that will be *all*," snapped Father.

He didn't care for the steward, but he didn't distrust him. To him, Willy Bede was a loyal servant who would never breathe a word of what he saw and heard in the great cabin. But to me, he was the perfect agent of a distant owner, the very man Mr. Goodfellow would choose to plant on the ship. I didn't speak again until he'd passed through the door, taking his big jug-handled ears beyond hearing. I looked at the chart, and the line of crosses that marked our progress toward Australia. The line curved and bent. There were more than a hundred and eighty crosses, marking that many days at sea, and it seemed that only a dozen more would connect the line to New South Wales.

"Father, please," I said. "Will you at least agree to help if you can?"

He answered my question with another. "Do you really think you're up to it, Tom?"

"Yes, sir," I told him.

"A boy from the city? A schoolboy?" He sighed. "You don't know the dangers in these islands."

"But we do!" cried Midge. "Don't that reverend tell it all? Didn't he say there's crocodiles and snakes?" His voice began to slur, as it always did when he got excited. "Eelsh and shpidersh. Ain't it all in the book?"

"That's nothing," said Father. "That isn't half of it. There are human dangers, too."

He held up a hand, fingers spread. "We won't even count the navy. But they'll go after you like a hound for foxes. They'll chase you day and night."

Father touched his index finger to count his first danger. "Headhunters, Tom. They paddle canoes as long as this ship. They'll take your heads for trophies." He touched the next finger. "Then there's the cannibals, and they're worse than the headhunters. They live here, and here," he said, jabbing at the islands on the chart. "Here and here, and maybe here as well. You can't tell by looking if they're cannibals or not. Each man you meet, you'll wonder: will he help you on your way or put you in a stew?"

There had been no cannibals in Midgely's book. Even the word put fear inside me.

"And if that's not bad enough," said Father, touching a third finger, "there's the pirates, the Borneo pirates."

His hand went again to the chart, down to the big sprawl of an island in the middle. "They go roving, Tom. Black ships with black sails. They'll take on a frigate, no fear. They

12

might slaughter the crew like so many sheep, or whisk them away to be slaves. Myself, I'd rather be killed."

I swallowed. It was as though he were talking of different islands from those in Midgely's book. The reverend had written of friendly natives, of whole villages turning out to greet him with dances and lavish feasts.

"Have you ever seen cannibals, Captain Tin?" asked Midgely.

Father shook his head.

"Have you seen headhunters? Or pirates?"

"No, William, but . . ."

"Then maybe they ain't there," said Midge. "Maybe *that's* the travelers' tales, and what the reverend said is the truth. He wouldn't lie, would he, Captain Tin?"

"You're willing to wager your life on it?" asked Father.

To my surprise, Midgely nodded. "We'd rather take our chance than be put in chains, and ain't that the truth, Tom?"

It seemed no choice at all. Seven years in chains would surely kill me. It would only be a slower, more miserable death.

"I admire your spirit," said Father. "But the problem remains. How can I set you off in a boat with nobody knowing?" He turned away from the table to stand again at his windows. The sea bubbled up from the stern, boiling into white streaks that faded away as we traveled on. "That's the crux of it, boys. Find an answer, and I'll do as you wish."

Midge and I went up to the deck and joined the convicts. As he always did when we left the cabin, Midgley winced and groaned and limped along, hoping the others would think he'd been punished. He thought he was awfully clever,

13

but there wasn't a soul who believed him. Though none really knew why we were called every fortnight to the captain's cabin, it was clear to all that Redman Tin would never lay a hand on anyone, and least of all on Midgely.

The sailors rounded up the convicts and marched us below. I stepped over the hatch with my usual sense of dread and despair. For all my father did to make the voyage bearable—with plenty of food and water, with a fiddler playing as we danced now and then—the ship was still a traveling prison, steaming hot or cold as frost. It stank of sweat and waste, and seethed with a simmering violence, like a cage overfilled with wild beasts. Among the sixty boys I had no friends but Midgely.

As we settled into our place, I watched Walter Weedle send a boy fleeing from his own spot near the hatch. His scar-split face made his grin seem huge. He sat like a little king, flanked by the other nobs who were his muscles and his bravery. That horrid Benjamin Penny was on his right, and the dim giant Gaskin Boggis on his left. Behind him was Carrots, and another called Early Discall.

Penny and Boggis and Carrots had belonged to the Darkey's gang. They had roamed through the streets of London together with my twin. After all our months at sea, it must have been plain to them that I was not the Smasher they had known, no matter how much I looked like him, and talked like him. We differed in nature so greatly that Father might have severed good from evil when he cut us apart on the stormy night of our birth. Yet Benjamin Penny, more than any other, would sit and stare at me—bewildered—as though trying to decide how a boy who had loved him could now de-

14

spise him so deeply. Ugly and freakish he was, but at times I nearly pitied him. Then I'd see him go at other boys, suddenly, with feet and fists and teeth. I'd hear the shrieks of his victims, and the soft thuds as Weedle sneaked in his cowardly blows, and then the bright shine in Benjamin Penny's eyes would turn me cold.

I watched them as they watched me, while the brig ran steadily east. Chased by storm and gale, we flew nothing but topsails for half a week, then no sails at all. We scudded bare-masted through a raging ocean, and then I trembled in the darkness. I hated the storms as much as Midgely loved them, and I was glad to have thoughts of escape to keep my mind from dwelling on the groans of the timbers, and the shaking of the masts.

When we were nine days from Australia, I still had no answer to the problem. Then the fates that had dogged me took a very strange turn.

There was a storm more vicious than any. It howled from dark to dawn, and down below we heard the lumber shifting on the deck, the mizzenmast being carried away. It left the decks in such a ruin that we were kept below through a full day and a night and a morning, then found the sailors still repairing damage.

Weedle and Carrots climbed up on the stacks of lumber. Benjamin Penny tried to go with them, but his twisted spine and wretched arms wouldn't let him scale the lumber. He tore shreds from the ancient, sun-rotted tarpaulins as he scuttled round and through the stacks, disappearing at one spot to emerge at another.

Midgely and I made our way to the stern. A new mast had

been fitted, and sailors were splicing the rigging. The carpenter was hammering away at the longboat, so we sat down to watch him, and were soon greeted by my father when he came up with his sextant. It was the first time he'd ever taken the deck when the convicts were free, and he was careful not to look down toward them. The sight of the boys, he'd said before, was enough to break his heart.

But he was happy to find Midgely and me. "Rotten weather, wasn't it?" he said. "Nearly tore the old ship apart, I tell you." He fiddled with the sextant, then held it to his eye. "We've been blown many leagues to the north. Do you see the clouds there on the horizon?"

I looked out and saw them in the north, flat clouds floating on the skyline.

"There's always land below clouds like that," said Father. "You may get to see your islands after all."

He squinted through the eyepiece as he worked the sliding arm. "Here, I was thinking of a dance," he said. "The boys enjoy a dance, don't they?"

"Very much," I said.

We watched him take the sight. Then he went below to work out the position, and we stayed with the carpenter. An old German, he muttered to himself as he drove strands of cotton rope between the longboat's planks.

"The fair battering she's tooken," said he. "The trouble she's made. But ach!" He rapped the hull. "Look, boys, fit as the fiddle again. Ve put her in the vater, and then you see, huh?"

"You're going to launch it now?" I asked.

"How else you sveeten planks?" said the carpenter.

16

"Vood, boy, it must to drink. Vood and men—ach!—they both the same."

He called for a crew, and the tackles were rigged, a towline attached. Then the longboat—with two pairs of oars lashed to its seats—was heaved over the side.

Midge squinted as he tried to see it all, then grinned at me. "All's Bob now," he said. "Ain't it, Tom?"

We went that day to my father with a plan. He would hold his dance, we said, when we were closer to the islands. And that night Midge and I would hide on deck instead of going below. "The sailors never count the convicts anymore," I said. "We'll hide in the stacks of lumber until you can bring us to your cabin. In the morning someone will say we're missing, and you'll say we must have drowned."

"Tom, they'll search the ship," said Father.

Midgely giggled. "High and low, but not in here 'cause *you'll* look here yourself. That's why it's rummy, Captain Tin."

"We can get out through your windows," I said. "The next night, or maybe the one after. We'll get into the longboat, and you can pass us food and water and charts of the island. We'll untie the rope, and everyone will think the boat got loose."

My father looked out through those windows. Just yards from where he stood, the longboat surged through the wake of the ship. "It's rather clever, by George," he said. "I could see to it that you'll steer due north to make landfall."

"Then we'll go on to the elephant island," said Midge. "We'll wait for you there."

"Yes." Father smiled. "What a happy accident, hmm? I'll

17

stop for water, and—good Lord!—there you'll be. You'll have to come aboard in chains, of course."

"I don't mind," said Midgely.

"Chains until we get to England," added Father. "Then we'll confront Mr. Goodfellow. Show him up for what he is."

Our plan seemed settled. But Midgely changed it all. "Wouldn't it be better if we hid aloft?" he said. "Instead of in the lumber, Captain Tin?"

I didn't like heights. I didn't want to climb the rigging, especially not in the dark. But Father agreed with Midge. "You're quite right, William. The maintop's a safer place."

And with those words, fate turned again.

three

A GHOSTLY VISIT

There were times I thought I'd been cursed. It seemed that, along with the wonderful diamond I had pulled from the Thames, I had picked up a devil as well. Midgely had told me once that my jewel might have been the famous Jolly Stone, the ruin of all who'd touched it. I had been plagued by such terrible luck, all my plans thwarted, that I dreaded the same would happen again.

But in the morning it seemed I had nothing to fear. From Father came word that a dance would be held that night, and the boys took off their caps and hurrahed.

All through the day the sea was flat, the wind a warm breeze. At noon a tower of rock appeared beyond the bowsprit, as though at the edge of the world. It looked like a bewitched bit of land, or a fabulous castle rising from the ocean. In the sunlight it shimmered.

Then slowly it collapsed. It settled into the water, and I realized that we'd seen a strange mirage, a twist and shatter of sunlight that had raised to our sights an island beyond the horizon.

I wondered what sort of omen this was.

The breeze faded away, and the ship—in a flap of sails and a groan of rope—wallowed on a bright, hot sea. The longboat lay motionless behind us. With no wind to hold them aloft, the albatrosses sat on the water. They looked like chickens laid out to fry on a white-hot griddle. The boys lay on their backs as though dead, looking up at the bleached canvas.

Late in the forenoon, clouds came riding from the east. They came in streaks and masses, like a cavalry of enormous yellow horses. Then a sailor arrived to take Midgely and me to the cabin.

We thought it was to settle our last plans. But we found Father by the windows, pacing back and forth. He told us straight out, "I've had a change of heart."

It was partly because of the weather. He didn't care for the calm and the clouds. "There's a storm brewing up," said he. "If it holds off till night, there's no fear. But if the wind picks up before sunset, it will blow like the very dickens."

"We ain't afraid," said Midgely.

"Of course you're not, William," said Father. "But . . ." He faltered and sighed. "Tom, I feel that I've been visited by your mother. I saw her as clear as day."

"Oh, Father," I said.

20

"She was in her veils and her shawls; she was right over there." He raised an arm and pointed. His finger was shaking. "There on my berth. She lay flat on her back."

"Well, that was Mother all right," I said dryly. For half my life I had known her to do little more than that. She had gone mad when my sister drowned. She had taken to her bed, and only rarely gotten up.

"She drew back her veils as I watched," said Father. "Her face was like ash. Even her lips were white. 'Keep him safe,' she told me. 'Keep the boy safe.' Then she faded away into nothing."

"Holy jumping mother of Moses. You're giving me the shivers," said Midgely. "She's on her deathbed, ain't she, Captain Tin? She's calling from her deathbed, she is."

I saw him do something he had never done before. He raised his little hand and crossed himself, touching his forehead, his lips, his breast, and shoulders.

I sat down then, though not on the bed. I fell into the chair by the table, feeling as though I were dropping into a bottomless pit. I found that I cared more for my mother than I'd ever thought, and the notion that she was now dying in her bed in England made me tremble through and through.

"Tom!" said my father. "Listen to me, Tom." He came beside me and lifted my chin. "She's not here, not in spirit nor in body. I was thinking of her, that was all. I know fully well— the both of us do—what she would say about you leaving the ship. Tom, I didn't see *her;* I saw my own thoughts."

"You're not going to let us escape, are you?" asked Midgely.

"No," said Father. "I'm not. I'll take you to Australia as I wanted. I'll explain it all to the governor, and I'll take you home again. That's what I've decided."

"Because of what you saw?" I asked.

"Because of what I *know*," said he. "You haven't got it in you, Tom. You're . . . well—dash it!—I'm sorry to say this, but you're too soft."

He turned away. He didn't go to the windows, but sat on the bed. He placed his elbows on his thighs, then settled his head in his hands. "It's not your fault, Tom; you've been coddled. Your mother worried too much."

His words stung more than he could know. It was true that I had been that way. I had been spoiled and selfish. But I believed I had changed, and it hurt me to think that my father couldn't see it.

Shadows spilled through the doorway. In crept old Bede, his long nose arriving first. "Would the young *convicts* . . . ," he started.

But Father's head snapped up, and he roared, "Get out, man! Leave us alone, you toad-eating fool."

Such anger I had never known from him. I saw the dismay on Bede's long face and—in that moment—I didn't believe he was a spy for Mr. Goodfellow. He couldn't have looked more injured if my father had taken a lash to him. Out he went, as stealthily as he'd arrived.

"Oh, Bede," Father called after him. "I'm sorry."

But it was too late. The man hadn't heard—or had chosen not to.

My father stood up. He moved behind me and put his hands on my shoulders. "Good Lord, I don't know what's wrong with me. I feel that I'm lying ahull today, beset by squalls. But, dear Tom, don't worry. I'll look after you."

I left the cabin nearly brokenhearted. Midge held my sleeve as we climbed up to the deck. "It's over now," I said. "I'll never get home."

"You might," said he. "You're the captain's son, ain't you? If he stands up for you, they might let you stay with him. He can do what he likes, a captain can."

What he said made sense, and—with that—my spirits lifted. We walked to the steps and down to the waist of the ship.

"I think he *will* get you home," said Midge. "But he can't help me. Not for spit."

I saw that he was crying. Down each cheek a tear was rolling, and the corners of his mouth were shaking. It broke my heart to see him so, for even when Benjamin Penny had punctured his eyes, Midge had never wept. He'd gone bravely on as a darkness engulfed him. But now it seemed his stuffing had been pulled away, and all that was left was a frightened boy. I wanted to tell him that if he had to stay in Australia that I would stay with him. But could I really do it? Would I pass up a chance to go home?

He sniffed. "At least I'll get to Australia. That's good, Tom; I'm glad for that. But I don't want to be there without you."

The strange calm lasted into evening. The air grew clammy hot, the sky full of clouds that looked torn and shredded, bleeding crimson through their wounds. My father had the topgallants furled, and reefs put in the topsails. He

23

ordered a sailor to double the length of the longboat's tow-line. But he kept to his word and let the convicts dance.

The fiddler sat where he always did, bobbing his black bush of a head as he squealed out cheerful songs. Boy danced with boy, convict with convict, in a wild confusion of stamping feet and swirling bodies. I saw the giant Gaskin Boggis whirling Penny by his webbed hands. The red hair of young Carrots was like a fire leaping through the crowd.

I had always loved our dances. They were moments of joy in months of misery. But now the music failed to stir me, and I sat with Midge at the foot of the main-mast shrouds.

The deck vibrated. The rigging trembled. Round went the boys in a lively reel, and their bare feet sent a drumroll over the sea and up to the sky, and it seemed to marshal the clouds. A breath of wind put a curl in the topsail; then the ship groaned from end to end.

"Here comes that storm," said Midge. "By cracky, don't your father know the sea?"

The next puff filled the mainsail. With a creak in her timbers, the ship started moving.

"It's Australia for me," said Midge. "If the wind pipes up they'll hoist the boat. They'd never tow it in a storm."

I heard the laughter of the sailors, the thumps as pairs of boys collided.

Midgely touched my arm. "Will you promise me something, Tom?" he asked. "When you get home, will you see if me mum's alive? And if she is, will you tell her I ain't angry that she didn't want me?"

"Oh, Midge," I said.

"Tell her this," said he. "Tell her, 'He got to go to sea, missus. Your boy went all the way to halfway round the world.' Will you say that to her?"

The ship was sailing now. The yards were braced, the deck aslant. Like sixty spinning tops, the convict boys massed along the lower rail.

I leapt up and grabbed Midgely. I pulled him to his feet; I danced him down the deck. We swirled among the boys and out again, past the lumber, past the fiddler. I pushed him against the mainmast shrouds. "Climb!" I told him.

He didn't question me. In a flash he was gone, scurrying up the ratlines. I followed him, but not so quickly. It alarmed me to feel the rope closing round my feet, the steep tilt of the ship. Before I was halfway up, the deck seemed impossibly distant. But I struggled on, and finally Midge reached down from the maintop and helped me through the lubber's hole. I collapsed on the broad, curved surface.

"Good for you, Tom," he said.

The top was more exposed than I'd thought it would be, nor as secure as I'd hoped. There was no rail or hoop to keep me there. I lay flat on my stomach, my hands wedged in the gap of the doubled mast. The big maincourse hung on its great yard, creaking as it shifted in the iron truss. I could look above it to the sails of the foremast, down to the dancing convicts. From side to side was empty sea.

The fiddler's song came to an end, and the dancing petered out. I looked for Boggis and Weedle and Benjamin Penny, but couldn't find them on the bit of deck that I could see. When the sailors marched the boys below, not one of the three, nor Carrots, was anywhere in the line.

25

"What are they up to?" I asked Midge. "Do you think they saw us? Do you think they know we're here?"

"Not a chance," said Midgely. "But even if they did, what does it matter?"

The wind kept rising as the sky grew dark. I looked out to the north, hoping to see the island we would have to reach, or at least the breakers on its shore. But there was not so much as a speck of land, and soon we were fully in darkness. The wind hummed; the maintop tilted as the brig bounded through the waves.

The air took on a hot tingle. Far away, lightning flashed and sizzled. Then the wind rose again, and a rain came driving down. It streamed from the sails above us, soaking the wood and soaking my clothes. The top became as slick as ice.

"Can you see the longboat?" Midgely asked. "Are they hauling it in?"

I turned around and peered from the back of the maintop. Lightning glared more closely, and I saw the helmsman at the wheel. I saw the longboat still behind us. Then the wind made a sudden shriek. The masts tilted far to the side, and I slithered across the wet top until my feet overhung the edge. We both held on—to the top and to each other—so that neither of us would go spinning off into the night.

Bolts of lightning smoked across the sky. I saw the sails glow with a pure whiteness, the rigging etched in silver. I saw a wave towering over the deck. Below me—in one instant—was only wild and boiling water, and in the next a shattered pile of wood. The stacks of lumber were breaking apart.

Then I saw Walter Weedle. I saw Carrots and Boggis, Benjamin Penny and Early Discall. Clasping hands, they stood in a human chain that stretched to the side of the ship. Weedle was anchored at the rail. Then the lightning seared again, and all of them were gone.

I thought they were lost. The truth was slow to sink in, but it did. I shouted at Midge, "They're taking the boat!"

I shifted around on the tilted top. Far behind and far below, I saw a feather of white spray where the longboat scythed back and forth on its towline.

What happened next I couldn't say. I knew only that Midgely was falling, that he'd somehow lost his balance. He slid past me and shot right over the edge. I grabbed his arm and clutched the shrouds, ready to take the shock of his weight. But it was too much, and it tore me from the rigging. We tumbled together, down past the mainsail and into the sea.

My canvas clothes buoyed me up. Bulges of air in the trousers and sleeves bobbed me to the surface. Midge was there, his hand still in mine. Waves tumbled over us, and spray stung our faces. As the ship sailed past, I began to struggle, and then to sink. It was little Midge who held me above the sea, but he couldn't hold on for very long.

four
ALL AT SEA

Something grabbed me in the water. It clutched me by the waist and tore me suddenly through the waves. My first thought was of a shark, the next of a whale that would swallow me whole. Whatever it was, it pulled me along at a frantic speed. Then it grabbed Midgely as well and pulled him, too. I saw the spray pluming from his hands and head as, side by side, we shot along across the sea.

I tried to fight the thing off, but wherever I pummeled and punched, my fists met only water. Then a low, dark shape went rushing by.

In a furious tumble of foam, it sliced down the back of a wave. It dove through the crest, then surfaced again, hurtling toward us.

It was the longboat, half on its side and half full of water.

Swinging out from the ship, it had dragged the towline with it. The rope was what held us, stretched tight as an iron bar.

As it veered across the wake, I reached out and grabbed the boat. It hauled me along, and I hauled Midge, our hands still locked together. He flailed and thrashed until he somehow got his own hand on the gunwale, and we hung on as the boat shot up the waves at a slant. I saw the ship—or at least the windows in the stern. They were squares of yellow light in a steeply slanted line, and in the middle was a figure, my father staring out. To him, the sea would be nothing but blackness, our struggle unseen.

A rumbling wave—a giant old graybeard—fell across us. With a bang, the tow rope snapped in two, and the longboat came to a stop. It rolled and wallowed in the waves, slopping water across the gunwales. Lighting flashed above us, and I saw my father's ship sailing along on her way.

Midgely and I clambered aboard the longboat, tumbling in turn over the side. I was shocked to see a face looking at me, a boy huddled in the stern. It was Walter Weedle, who had vowed to kill me, and once nearly had. But now he was sobbing, his eyes wide with fright. The long scar that split his face from ear to ear writhed like a white worm.

"They're gone," he said. "They're all drownded, every one."

We bailed out the boat with our hands. I told Weedle to help, but he only stared at me blankly, as though he didn't hear or couldn't understand. The storm bore away to the east in fading blinks of lightning. It carried the wind along with it, and the rain with its rumble of drops, and left us again, drifting in the moonlight.

The oars were still lashed to the seats. So was the rudder and tiller, but otherwise the boat was empty. We had no food or water, neither knife nor gun, not even a flint to strike a fire. We had come from a ship that had been a world in itself, to a shell of a boat with not a single thing to keep us alive.

Suddenly Weedle stood up. He set the boat rolling as he stared out at the sea. "Did you hear that?" he cried.

We had heard no sounds.

"They was calling for me," said Weedle in a whisper. "They was calling my name."

I thought he'd gone mad. But then I heard the voices myself. Faintly, ghostly, they cried out for help.

I worked at the lashings to free the rudder and a pair of oars. I grabbed Weedle by the collar and hauled him down to the seat. "Row!" I told him.

I had to fit the pins myself, and place the oars between them. Then, as he rowed, I fitted the rudder and tiller. I steered toward the cries.

Out of the night came Benjamin Penny, swimming fast and froglike, with such strength that he might have swum all the way to Australia if he'd cared to. His webbed hands reached up and grabbed the gunwale, and he swung himself into the longboat. We found the others clinging to a raft of lumber, and brought them aboard. Then, seven in number, we rowed in a direction that I hoped was north. I could see none of the stars that I'd known in England.

I would gladly have seen Weedle rowing forever. But he was so useless that Early Discall asked to take his place. "Never rowed no boat," he said. "But who could do worse than that?"

Yet he did, at first. He twisted the oars and toppled himself from the seat. Laughing at his own clumsiness, he got up and tried again, and soon was rowing like an old boatman, singing away at the top of his voice. It was a plowman's tune that he piped out, in a high-pitched tone that broke off—now and then—into a deeper voice. I found Early to be a very pleasant fellow; I liked him right away.

Boggis sat smiling stupidly, and Benjamin Penny curled up like a rat in a hole. Midgely leaned against me on the seat at the back, with the big tiller between us, and through the night we traveled on. Early told us stories of his west-country home, in his west-country accent that was full of strange words and phrases. When Weedle began to complain of the cold, Early told him to stop his "crewnting."

At first light we saw the island. By what I thought was a great stroke of luck, it lay right before us, the tiny tip of a great, rocky mountain. But it wasn't the only thing on the sea.

Far behind us were the sails of a ship. Made tiny by distance, they were stacked like wooden building blocks on the hard edge of sea and sky. It could have been any ship at all, but I didn't doubt it was my father's.

"Stop rowing," I said. "Everyone sit still." If I could see the sails, then a lookout could see us as well. So we sat and drifted, in the warming sunrise, soaring on the swells. Up we rushed, and down again, in such a swooping rhythm that I felt the seasickness crawling back inside me.

The distant ship went east and west, the sails steadily shrinking. I imagined my father frantically searching the sea. I was certain that he would be the one at the masthead, training his spyglass all around. It gave me a very lonely feeling when the ship finally vanished toward the south. I told Early to row.

Weedle scowled. "Who made *you* the captain?"

I shouldn't have been surprised, as he had always craved power over others. Now he puffed himself up like a rooster, and crowed, "Look here. This boat's mine, by rights. Weren't I the first one in it?"

Midgely laughed. "You was blubbering like a baby."

"You shut up!" snapped Weedle. "You're worse than useless, you are."

Midgely trotted out that silly saying of boys. "Does your mother know you're out?" he said, sounding smug and tart.

It was a nonsensical remark, but it seemed to enflame Walter Weedle. His long scar pulsed, and his eyes shrank to black coals. It was a look that had terrified me in the hulk, before I'd found that there was more bark than bite to the boy. But now his fury scared me again.

Weedle was in the bow, and between us sat Carrots and Benjamin Penny, the giant, and Discall. It seemed to be five against two, in an open boat on the empty sea. In a flash they could be on us. They could throw Midgely and me over the side, and who would ever know?

Benjamin Penny smiled. He cackled softly, and I could see that the same thoughts had occurred to him. There was pleasure in his look, a wicked expectation.

Gaskin Boggis stared stupidly over the sea, but the rest of us sat staring in our places, all leaning to the right as the boat soared up and over a wave. Then Weedle stood up.

"Here, we're done with rowing," said Weedle. "It's your turn, Tom, don't you think?"

Early Discall piped up that he didn't mind rowing. But Weedle told him to keep quiet. "Tom's going to row us to the island," he said. "That's as far as he has to go. He'll be getting a long rest after that."

Boggis was too thick to see the meaning in that. "We're staying there?" he asked.

"Only Tom and his little mollycoddle," said Weedle. "We'll be going along without them."

Beside me, Midgely scoffed. "*Go along!* Where do you think you're going along *to*, Walter Weedle? You can't even say where you *are*."

The look that came to Weedle's face was almost comical. He couldn't have given the slightest thought to where he'd go from the ship. He had only fled from it mindlessly, like a bird from an open cage.

"It's only Tom and me what knows the way," said Midgely. "We seen the charts. We learnt the islands in a book."

"Midge, that's enough," I said. But it was too late.

"You know the way to *where*?" asked Weedle.

"To the ship!" cried Midge. "We're meeting the ship, you stupid, and it's taking us home."

He let a thousand cats from a thousand bags with those few words. Weedle was still on his feet, rocking like a skittle with the maddening roll of the boat. He took a step forward. "What ship's that?"

"Why, the one what we left, of course," said Midge. "How else could we plan it?"

"You hear that, lads?" said Weedle, looking about. "Is that what you want, to get back on the ship?"

Early shook his head, and Gaskin rather rumbled in his chest. "I ain't going back," he said.

"Hold him!" shouted Weedle. "Hold Tom Tin."

In a moment, the giant had me in his grasp. Weedle rushed past him. He pitched little Midgely from the seat, then kicked me hard in the chest. "*Now* you'll row," he said. "Another word, and it's your last."

Perhaps we were caught up in the currents of fate, and no matter what I'd said or done we would have ended on that island to the north. As it was, I broke my back to get there, and within the hour it was clear that the island was a small and terrible place. The tip of gray stone wasn't a mountaintop in the distance. It was all there was of a lonely speck of land, a misery of earth and rock not much bigger than my father's ship, nor half as high as the masts. There was not a tree or bush, not a single thing that looked alive. From end to end, from shore to summit, it was covered in white, as though coated impossibly with snow.

I described it for Midge, hoping he would name the place. But he said the reverend writer had never seen a white island by itself. "We ain't in the book yet, Tom," said Midge. "That's the trouble."

I hadn't imagined we would have to find our way into the book. This merely added to my growing dread as we came closer to the island. I thought what a lonely prison it was about to make for Midge and me. A prison for a while, and a terrible tomb forever.

When we were half a mile off, we saw other islands far beyond it. Faint and blue, like smudges of clouds, they barely poked above the horizon. For a moment it cheered me, for this first bit of rock seemed a little less lonesome. But then I thought of the horror of always looking at land we could never reach.

"Row!" shouted Benjamin Penny. He kicked sharply at my ribs.

I pulled on the oars. Suddenly, from the island, came a fluttering and a roar, and it seemed that the rocks themselves lifted up and took to the air, blasting in every direction. It was a flock of birds, such a mass that they had covered every inch of the island, and now swirled round and round above it. The rocks turned in the instant from white to speckled black. But the crag itself seemed even smaller without the birds, and the cloud of them was enough to darken the sky. Then we heard the sound of their wings, a rumble like thunder, and the screeching cries of their voices.

And I saw, on a jagged ridge, a man running.

He leapt to a knoll and vaulted to another, stumbled and rose and kept running. He ran as though his life depended on it, ran like a frightened deer, hurdling rocks and leaping chasms. Over the slope he went, his arms flailing, then turned and disappeared behind the ridge.

five

THE WRECK OF THE LONGBOAT

No one but me saw the running man. As quickly as he'd appeared, he vanished again. I might have thought I hadn't seen him at all, only a strange pattern in the swirl of wings and feathered bodies. But something had surely set those birds into flight, so I didn't doubt I had seen the figure, as unsettling as it was.

What made that man flee so desperately, as though his life hung in the balance? It seemed that a glimpse of us had set him running in terror. But why?

His island was broken and craggy, besieged on all sides by the sea. It was overcome with such a sense of gloom that I wondered if Weedle might change his mind, and not land there at all. In his place, I would have kept going to the farther, greener places. Or so I told myself. In truth, I hadn't stood on solid land for more than half a year, and I longed to get off the sea.

Weedle looked far from happy now. He glowered at the island as he steered us west-about around it, looking for a place to land. But all along the shore, waves burst into creamy froth, and towers of spray shot high in the air. On the weather side were cliffs and caves, and the sea was at its wildest. In the middle, the island narrowed to a short and steep-sided neck, so that it took on the shape of a pair of squashed spectacles. The neck was filled with jumbles of rock, piled stone upon stone, and looked a most treacherous spot. On the eastern shore were reefs and splintered rocks.

All this time, the birds soared round above us. The flash and whirr of thousands of wings reminded me of raging water, of eddies and whirlpools. It reminded me how all my luck ran against me.

"I don't like this place," said Boggis. "It's haunted, I think." And Early agreed.

I didn't believe in ghosts, but the island had the same effect on me. With the waves slamming against it, and the screaming birds flitting their shadows across the rock, the place seemed restless and besieged. I watched for the running man, and wondered why he wasn't down at the water already, begging us to take him off.

"Please, Weedle," said Boggis. "Go on to them other islands. You ain't never steered a boat. You don't know how to land it."

He might as well have waved a red rag at a bull. "We'll see about that," said Weedle. He cursed and told me to row faster. "That's where we'll land, right there."

I glanced over my shoulder, to see where he was pointing. It was a narrow gap between pillars of rock, where the sea reared up in an enormous bulge of green water. Then, swollen and seething, it hurled itself between the pillars and over their tops, filling a great basin beyond them. In that space the sea tumbled and writhed, and up shot geysers of white water.

I rowed for all I was worth, but only with one oar. I spun the boat around.

Too late I'd tried to save us. The sea already had a hold of the boat. It swept us toward the gap, and the sound of the surf grew loud as cannons. Weedle looked as though he were staring at death, and his hand was white on the tiller.

Then we rose on that bulge of water, and for an instant it seemed that all was still and quiet. Higher we went, until we looked over the rocks and into the black-sided basin. I heard the rattling rush of an undertow sucking at pebbles and stones.

"It's Tom's fault!" screamed Weedle.

There was nothing that could save us. The boat was carried straight into the gap as we clung to its sides. The bow struck a boulder, and splinters of wood went flying. One of my oars snapped in two. The sides of the boat rippled and cracked as we jammed between the rocks like a bung in a barrel. The stones rumbled in the suck of the sea as the wave fell away below us. But the next came thundering behind it, lifting the boat by the stern, prying it free from the boulders. A thwart split down the middle; the tiller went flying; and the longboat flipped end over end, flinging us all into the sea.

I landed on the beach. Midgely fell beside me, and a

wave swept over our heads. I pushed him high up the beach, then held on to the stones as the undertow sucked me back. I saw Early tumbling down in the surf, and Gaskin hurry to help him. Weedle, Carrots, and Benjamin Penny were scrambling for the shore. With no thought for the boat or anyone else, they pulled themselves up to the sheltering cliffs. I ducked my head as the water came surging over the boulders again.

It left us half drowned, coughing for breath. But I pulled Midgely along, and Boggis dragged Early. The poor longboat rolled over and over. Caught by the undertow, it was pulled down in the basin, and vanished completely in the boiling water. Then suddenly it rose, stern first, as though spat like a fruit pit from the sea. It broke clear from the water, held by its end in a white fist of spray. Then it turned slowly in the air, and came crashing down on a high ledge of black stone.

Below it we huddled at the edge of the water. Early seemed in a daze, as though he couldn't believe what had happened. It was no wonder, really; we sprawled in a staggered row, on an island that had no name, with the wreckage of our boat tumbling at our feet.

Weedle was already at the top of the cliffs. He stood there and cursed me. He shouted oaths I'd never heard, and damned my eyes and damned my soul. "What now?" he asked. "What now, Tom Tin?"

I wanted to rest. I wanted to lie in the sun the whole day long, then sleep on dry land that didn't heave and shift underneath me. But instead I got to my feet and began to collect the bits of flotsam that came cartwheeling up on each wave.

With the surf pounding, and the spindrift flying, I staggered up and down the little stretch of beach, for the land felt anything but steady. It seemed to tilt and rock more wildly than boat or ship had ever done.

Boggis worked beside me. We salvaged two oars, a piece of another, a shattered plank and a broken thwart. We found the rudder, but not the tiller, a curve of the stem, and a chunk of the transom. We carried it all to the longboat, and threw it down inside. There seemed little chance the boat would ever float again, but I put on a brave face for Midge, telling him that a bit of work would set it straight. If he knew I was lying, he didn't let on.

We struggled up the cliffs. Gaskin had to carry Early Discall, who—still in his daze—walked like a teetering, drunken man. At the top was a path worn in the ground, scuffed through gravel and dirt. It soon forked, leading in one direction to the middle of the island, and in the other to a rocky pillar that stood alone like a castle's turret. There was even a narrow bit of cliff—like a drawbridge—that had to be crossed to reach it. There, Weedle and the others had found a small cave, and a trickle of water that smelled rather foully of sulfur. But I was parched, and the water looked like silver to me.

When we started out on the narrow ridge, Weedle called to us to stop. "Find your own water," he said. "There ain't enough here for all of us."

"There might not be any more," I said.

His scar gleamed. "More's the pity then, ain't it?"

"At least give us some for Early," I said. "He'll die without it."

"He'll die anyway," said Benjamin Penny. "He's off to his Early grave."

Weedle laughed. So did Carrots, though it sounded loud and false.

"Put him down, Gaskin, and come here," said Weedle. "There's water enough for you."

The giant seemed torn. He took a step toward Weedle, then a step away, and turned himself fully about with Early on his back. "I can't just leave him, Weedle," he said. "I don't know what to do."

In the end he came along with Midge and me, trekking over the island. The birds muttered and squawked, then flurried away before us in a flap of wings. Each one we disturbed moved into the mass of others, disturbing more itself, so that the whole ground seemed to ripple and shift in our path.

On the island's low summit I found the first signs of the running man: a flattened space with a handprint in the dirt; a scattering of broken seashells.

I looked over the sea at the faraway islands, five little cones on the northern horizon.

Gaskin's breath went out in a heavy sigh. He lowered Early to the ground and sat beside him, staring to the north. "How far are them islands?" he asked.

It was a simple problem of angles and distance, one that I would have solved in a moment with a slate and a chalk. But I'd been too long away from my classes, and it made my head spin to figure it out.

From a hundred feet above the sea, how far was the horizon? I closed my eyes to think. Thirteen miles or so; could that be right? Unless the islands were impossibly tall, they couldn't be more than twenty miles distant.

What did it matter, though? Without a boat we were doomed.

I sat there at the summit. On the ground was a pyramid of tiny pebbles, a small feather stuck in the top like a flag. I imagined our wildman building it, pebble by pebble, as he watched for a sail on the sea. Had the watching driven him mad, I wondered?

Midgely looked up, and I knew we would learn the truth in a moment. We heard a crunching on the path, then footfalls on the stone.

Six
A FIGURE IN GREEN

The wildman came toward us, stepping up along the trail. I saw the birds shifting ahead of him, a wave of white rising from the ground and spreading apart, as though he kicked his way through banks of snow. He came up the slope and round a corner, muttering away a mile a minute.

"We'll find them up 'ere," I heard him say. "They'll be sitting at the lookout."

Then he came fully into view, a strange figure in very strange clothes. He didn't look as wild as he had on the ridge, though his face was bearded, his hair long and bedraggled. On his head he wore a rounded hat—a helmet—the color of seaweed. His jacket and his ragged trousers were of the same green hue, each made of many tiny pieces crudely stitched together, overlapping one another. It gave him the appearance of a sea creature, a merman scaled like a fish.

At his waist, from a leathery belt, hung an axe. Its handle had broken and split, and was now very short, but I thought it was all that separated the man from utter savagery. Then I looked down and saw his shoes. Too big by four sizes, their tops gaped open, and twisted sinews took the place of long-vanished laces. How he could have run so nimbly while wearing those was more than I could imagine.

He kept muttering. "See? Told you so," said he. "Said we'd find them 'ere." His hand touched and stroked his hair.

His eyes had the sparkle of a young man's, but the skin around them was cracked with crow's-feet. Three fresh scratches ran down his cheek and into his beard. He reached up to his hair, and I saw movement there, a shape, then a face.

I nearly cried out in surprise. Clinging to his matted hair was a little creature. For a moment I thought it was a bird, a nearly black and bone-thin bird. But then it peered out at me, and I saw the face and pointed ears of a small brown bat.

It was to that creature, and not himself, that he was talking. "Why, they're only boys," he said. "Do you see that, Foxy? Only boys."

The bat let out a shrill little murmur. It was clinging upside down in the fellow's hair, its horrible feet hooked on the helmet rim. By the way it moved, drawing upward, I guessed that it had been licking the blood from those fresh scratches.

The man laughed, as though the bat had answered with a clever riposte. Then he turned his twinkling eyes onto us and said, with a bow, "I'm Lord Mullock."

"You're a *lord*?" I asked.

"And more," said he. "Hah! You could never imagine."

He showed none of the joy I might have expected. Shouldn't he have capered about or danced a jig to find other people on his lonely island? All he did was look at us in a wary sort of way, as though he owned riches that he suspected we'd hoped to plunder.

"Out with it, now," he said. "Where 'ave you come from?"

I saw no reason to lie. "We're convicts," I said. "We escaped from a ship."

"Escaped?" The bat swung in his hair as he turned his head. "You hear that, Foxy? They escaped to 'ere!" He cackled a laugh. "Hah! Now, my boy, you must be thanking the living saint that led you to this speck of God's good earth. Well, thank 'im today, for you'll curse 'im tomorrow. Oh, you'll curse 'im soon enough, you'll see."

He said this in a friendly fashion, in an accent like none I'd heard. Whatever he was, he was not a lord; of that I was certain. He was clearly a man who shaped his words to sound as he imagined a lord should sound. The result was like a poor mimicry of Mr. Goodfellow, with the addition of a strange and unlordly habit with *h*s. He dropped them from the front of words, and tacked them instead onto others. "Now, what hunspeakable crimes 'ave you done?" he said.

Midgely was quick to answer. "It was only buffing dogs for me, sir. I killed them for their skins, was all. But Tom Tin here . . ." His voice swelled with pride. "For Tom it was *murder*."

"Hah! A murdering boy," said the man. "Now, what do you make of that, Foxy?"

45

I wanted to explain that I was innocent, but the man gave me no chance. "Where's your boat?" he asked. "You didn't land at Sheerness. You didn't come up by the Thames, I know that."

Well, he *was* loonie. Sheerness was in England. It was where the prison hulk had been moored, and where my voyage had begun. The poor fellow must have imagined himself on an island as big as Britain with rivers and cities and all. I pointed and told him, "The boat's wrecked on the shore over there."

A little sound came from his throat. "Wrecked?"

"In splinters," said I.

"Hah!" His head shook unbelievingly, his green helmet flopping from side to side. He made another choking sound, then laughed quite loudly—at the irony of it, I supposed. "Why, what else could it be but wrecked? What else hindeed?"

"Will you help us?" I asked. "Our friend here's hurt and he needs water. But the others . . ."

"How many others?"

"Three," I told him. "They found the pool and . . ."

"That stinky place," added Midgely.

"They wouldn't let us near it," I said.

"Hah! At each others' throats already, are you?" asked our "lord" Mullock. "Well, that's the *baths,* you poor, besotted boys. You don't want to be drinking from that."

"Is there other water, m'lord?" asked Midgely.

A wonderful smile came to that bearded face. "Of course there's other water. But don't lord me round," said the man. "No need for that 'ere. To you I'm *Mister* Mullock, and that's good enough." He'd clearly taken to Midgely, and gave him a friendly pat. "Now, what's wrong with your friend?"

"He hit his head when we landed," I said.

"He's bleeding," said Boggis. "There's a big lump behind his ear."

"Heggs!" shouted Mr. Mullock.

"What?" I said.

"It's heggs 'e needs, not water. Heggs will save 'im."

Mr. Mullock waded in among the birds. He chased them off with his arms waving, then plucked from the ground a dozen small green eggs. Of these, he gave one to each of us, then piled the rest beside Early, and knelt to feed the boy. He cracked each egg on the ground, and touched to Early's lips the little green chalice of shell. Early spat up the first one, and nearly choked on the second, but the change that came over him was remarkable. After four eggs he had stopped his trembling and was sitting upright, greedily feeding the rest to himself, pushing them whole into his mouth, crunching the shells in his teeth.

Yet there was something strange about him. I didn't know what it was, except that he asked no questions. Here he was, sitting with a bearded man who had a helmet on his head and a bat in his hair, but he didn't so much as blink his eyes. He just sat there chewing eggs.

Gaskin Boggis looked relieved. For such a huge boy, so easily angered, he had a surprising tenderness. He smiled at Early, then got slowly to his feet. "I'd better go back," he said. "Weedle, he'll be hopping mad."

"Who's Weedle?" snapped Mr. Mullock "Is 'e one of the boys at the baths?"

"Yes," I said. "He likes to give orders."

"Hah!" Mr. Mullock reached up for Gaskin's arm. "You tell them this, you great cabbage. Tell them not to go wandering. It's not a safe place for boys who wander about; is it, Foxy?"

The bat squeaked. It held on to a thick curl of the man's hair, its little eyes like black beads. Mr. Mullock didn't seem so friendly now. Such a change had come over him, so quickly, that it made me cringe inside.

"The same happlies to all of you," he said. "Stay out of the caves and away from the wall. Whatever you do, don't hever cross the wall."

"But we ain't found no wall," said Midgely.

"Then don't go looking, mind," said Mr. Mullock. "But if you 'appen to find one, don't think of breaching it." His voice was low and menacing. "There's no telling what might get out if you did. I believe there's a Gypsy back there."

It was a long while since Mr. Mullock had been as young as us. I guessed he'd forgotten that to tell a boy not to think of something was enough to brand the notion in his head. As for his Gypsy . . . well, many a time my mother had tried to scare me with such warnings. On her list of frights, Gypsies had been only lower than chimney sweeps, and at six I'd lived in terror of them both. But now I had the sense to know that a rock on the ocean was fairly safe from Gypsies.

Not so for Gaskin, it seemed. Not so for him or Midgely. I saw worry come over their faces, and they cast furtive glances over the island. Then Gaskin stepped back. "I'd better hurry," he said.

I suddenly didn't want him to go, and not for any thought

of Gypsies. I wished only that he was a friend to me instead of Weedle. "You can stay with us if you like," I told him.

"Golly," he said. "Thank you, Tom." A blush came to his face, and he looked down in shyness. It was as though no one had ever offered such a thing before. "But that's where I should be, ain't it?" he said.

With that he went away, slouching down the path. Early watched him go, then cracked another egg and said, "Seems a nice fellow, that one. Not too fitty, but fore-right, eh? Has he been longful on the island?"

Midgely gaped. "What do you mean?"

"Oh, nothing more," said Early, shrugging. "I like him, that's all. Big bruiser, though, ain't he?"

It was clear that Early had no memory, that he'd forgotten everything he'd ever seen or done. For him, it seemed, there had never been an England, never crime nor punishment, only this tiny island and a few people of whom he knew nothing.

Mr. Mullock understood it too. "You've lost your recollections, boy," he said. "You've had a bump on the noggin."

Early touched his head, and felt the swelling there. "Strike me dead!" he cried. "So I have."

"Well, never mind, lad," said Mr. Mullock, all kindness again. "We'll 'elp you along." He pointed at me. "You—Tom, is it?—you're 'is size, more or less. Prop 'im up, and follow me."

I gave him a dark look that he didn't see. Nothing annoyed me more than a lazy fellow; it was what had come from having a mother who'd lain flat out all the day long. But I did as he asked, and we started for the southern end of the island. Instead of leading the way, Mr. Mullock trailed behind, calling out directions—"Turn left at that rock. Straight down the 'ill now."

The thunder of surf fell away, and the wind rustled in the feathers of the birds. Early kept an arm around my shoulders and leaned his weight against me.

"Hurry!" shouted Mr. Mullock, which annoyed me even more.

"You might show us the way," I told him.

"No, no," said he. "You'll 'ave no trouble when we get to the City. Just follow the Strand, and we'll take Blackfriar's bridge."

"You're mad," I muttered to myself. How could a man, no matter how long he'd been alone, imagine London laid out on his island. "You must know the City," I said.

"Know it? I built it!" said he. "I'm the Lord Mayor of London, my boy. Every building, brick, and stone I put in place myself. Now turn right, and you'll find the fountain."

We came to a place where the birds gathered more thickly than ever. They didn't move aside until my feet and my shins pushed them bodily away. Then I saw water bubbling from the stone, a knob of water that stood above the ground and shimmered red from the sunset, like a bright flame trembling.

"This is the 'eadwaters 'ere," said Mr. Mullock. "All of the Thames rises from this."

It was a trickle, but he thought it a river. Where I saw only rock, stained with black fingers of wetness, he saw the marshes and lakes of England.

"On you go," he said. "Cross the heath and down to the City."

We passed round a boulder. Then we stood at the top of a slope, and I couldn't believe what I saw. Below me lay all of London.

It was built of stones and seashells, of pebbles and sand. Every building and bridge, every street and steeple was there. On my left was Buckingham Palace, and there ahead was the Tower, and Mr. Mullock's narrow Thames flowed past all the places that I knew. In a glance I could see where I had blundered in the yellow fog on the first day of my long adventure. I could see where I'd met the blind man, and wrestled with him for the enormous diamond. I could trace, for a distance, the route that I'd taken with old Worms, in his cart pulled by a three-legged horse. But I couldn't follow it all the way to the churchyard where we had unearthed my dead twin from his grave. Mr. Mullock's London became blurred and indistinct the farther it stretched from the center. In a strange fashion, I was looking into his mind, seeing the clarity of things he knew well, and the vague memories of others.

It was plain that he had known the clubs and cathedrals, the banks and Exchange, and very little beyond Cheapstreet. He had known—in truth—just the very parts that a real lord might have known. My opinion of him changed somewhat, and he became even more of a mystery.

I lingered too long above London. In a great huff, Mr. Mullock suddenly passed me. He took Midgely by the arm and marched him down the Strand, like a giant who strode half a mile in one step. The high dome of St. Paul's reached almost to his knee, its round top recreated by the burnished shell of an enormous clam. With Early Discall leaning on my shoulder, I slowly fell farther behind as I gazed round at the miniature city. I rubbed a knee on the Parliament buildings, and nearly toppled the spire of St. Mary's.

Then Mr. Mullock called out, "Look lively. Over the bridge and east we go."

It was the route to Chatham that we took, the road that had taken me from London to the hulk. There was a church I remembered glimpsing from the window of my coach, then only scattered buildings, and vast and empty places, until we came to a crowded tangle of grim, square buildings. It could only be the Woolwich dockyards, though I couldn't imagine how a lord might know them.

It marked the end of his remembered world. Beyond that was nothing but the natural rocks of the island, and in a few steps we came to another cliff. His Thames tumbled there, down a thin cataract to a wonderful beach in a little cove where the sea was clear and placid. Yards from shore, the sea smashed on a line of rock and boulders, and I understood how we'd passed the place without seeing it.

"Sheerness!" announced Mr. Mullock. "If you'd landed 'ere, you would 'ave 'ad no trouble. But no, you 'ad to make your hentrance at Land's End, didn't you? You wrecked on the Cornish coast, you fools."

The bat was crawling through his hair. It moved in a slow and ghastly fashion, hanging upside down as it slithered to his shoulder. In a shrill little chatter, it cried out.

"Hah!" said Mr. Mullock. "Mind your tongue now, Foxy. There'll be no more of that."

"No more of what?" I asked.

Mr. Mullock glared at the bat, then looked sideways at me through tangled forelocks. "Death, he means. Death and dying. Hah! What else do bats ever think of?"

seven
MR. MULLOCK'S JUSTICE

Mr. Mullock made his home on that bit of the island between London and Sheerness. Overlooking his little harbor was a cave, and across its entrance hung slabs of fish that dangled from a leather string. It was the darkest of caves, booming with the sound of the sea. Somewhere beneath us, the swells rolled right into the rocks.

Despite his warnings to stay away from the caves, Mr. Mullock led us straight through the entrance, parting the fish like a curtain. We stepped into total darkness.

I heard Mr. Mullock working nearby, but couldn't see a thing. A loud clang echoed through the chamber, and a flurry of sparks flew close to the ground. There was another clang, a squeal from the bat, and an oath from the man. Then Mr. Mullock seemed to coax fire from the earth itself, breathing his sparks into flames. When the cavern brightened I saw him crouched in the middle, with foul-smelling smoke rising round his shoulders. He'd set alight a pool of oil in a chipped-away groove, and now—from that—lit several little bowls that he wedged around the walls.

The cavern was so huge that the light from the lamps barely reached the farthest wall. It left black holes to mark where tunnels led farther into the rock, and I guessed that the island was a honeycomb of passages. The room where we sat was stuffed with barrels. Some were big and others small, and they stood in stacks, in piles and rows, everywhere I looked. It was a pirate's hoard of treasure, I thought. But when I looked more closely I saw that they weren't really barrels. They were the shells of giant turtles. Along the side by the entrance, they stood like a line of green breastplates, the armor of Neptune's soldiers. Then I understood why Mr. Mullock looked so strange. His clothes were turtle skin; his helmet had been fashioned from a shell. He had made dozens of bags from the bodies or guts of the creatures, and the bowls of his lamps from the shells. His cavern was a turtle tomb, filled with the remains of so many animals that I couldn't imagine how long it had taken to collect them. No wonder he conversed with a bat.

Mr. Mullock fed us fish. He gave us water, and a crude liquor that was heavy and thick, unlike anything I'd tasted before. I didn't care for it at all—it was brewed from turtle blood, I thought—and secretly tipped my bowl down a fissure.

"You'll all sleep 'ere, of course," said Mr. Mullock. "In the morning we'll float your boat round to Sheerness and get 'er up in the navy yards."

"It might be beyond saving," I said.

"Time will tell." He slurped from his bowl. "We'll 'ave to see 'ow Fate plays 'er 'and."

It was strange to hear my own thoughts echoed by this fellow. But even stranger was Early's next question. He looked at me and asked, "You came here by boat, did you?"

"We all did," I said. "You were with us, Early."

"Was I really?" His brow wrinkled—from doubt or worry; I couldn't tell. "Then I must be a dawcock. Have I been here longful myself?"

"No," said Midge. "I'll tell you how it happened." He shuffled across the floor, then began to tell Early all that the boy had forgotten. His soft voice murmured away as the sea boomed in the depths of the island.

"Tom, where's 'e from, that boy?" asked Mr. Mullock.

"I don't know," I said. "Devon, I think. He talked about Bristol."

"Hah! Might be anywhere from Coventry to Timbuctoo for all 'e knows." Mr. Mullock touched his own temple. "The bang on 'is nut's made 'im stupid, you know. Whatever 'e says, it's bound to be nonsense."

Mr. Mullock talked through the evening and into the night. He asked about me, about Midge, about Gaskin and the others. With the food and the fire, the moan of the wind, I felt desperately tired. I answered each question with fewer words, then with only nods and grunts. Finally I fell asleep, not to wake until daylight.

The cave was quiet then, and the smell of cooked eggs stirred me awake. It was such a wonderful smell that I lay for a while with my eyes closed, wishing when I opened them that I would find myself at home in London, all my adventures only a dream.

The thought took my mind to my father. I imagined him hurrying to Australia, his ship flying with every sail set. All at once, a hundred fears came over me. Did he believe that I had drowned; did he know that I'd escaped? Would he still head for Midgely's elephant island? How long would it take him to get there, and how long would he wait for us? We had to fix the boat. We had to find that place.

It seemed that there was not a moment to spare. In a shot I was up, expecting to find Mr. Mullock cooking the eggs. But it was Early Discall who labored over the little fire of burning oil. Mr. Mullock was lying in the sunshine, on his ledge, at the mouth of the cave.

"Where's Midgely?" I asked.

Early pointed to the entrance. In the smoke he squinted terribly.

But Midge wasn't on the ledge. "Oh, I sent 'im off," said Mr. Mullock. "He's gone to fetch the water."

"You sent a blind boy for water?" I asked.

He nodded. "Yes. A smart lad, that one. Terrible, 'ow 'e lost 'is eyes, hisn't it?"

I could hardly believe his laziness. He didn't shift as Midge came staggering round the rocks with one of the big turtle-gut bags slung across his shoulders. He didn't move at all until he'd finished his breakfast, except to pluck bits of chewed egg from his mouth and feed them to the bat.

When we trekked toward the longboat, the island seemed

deserted. The thousands of birds that had covered it were gone, and only a few fledglings remained, squawking from their nests as we passed. Mr. Mullock said every day was the same. The birds left with the dawn, scattering themselves all over the sea.

Their absence made for a quicker passage, and we were soon scrambling down the cliffs on the western shore. We found the longboat there, high and dry, just as we'd left it the day before.

"She's not so bad," said Mr. Mullock, eyeing it over. "A couple of planks, a few nails 'ere and there, new ribs and a knee; that's all she needs."

It sounded like a great deal to me. "Just where will we get all that?" I asked.

"Hah! No fear there," said Mr. Mullock. "I'm Lord of the Hadmiralty too."

The waves still tumbled through the gap, and the pebbles rolled and rattled in the undertow. But the sea was much calmer in the channel between the island and its reefs, and we had no trouble launching the boat. Even Mr. Mullock lent a hand, kicking the loose bits of wood across the beach as the dreadful Foxy dangled from his hair. We slid the hull across the stones, and the rumble it made must have alerted Weedle, who appeared at the clifftop with Benjamin Penny.

"Ahoy there, Mr. Turtle Man," he called down at us. "You won't get far in that, you silly coot."

"Well, hisn't 'e the clever one?" said Mr. Mullock. The hull was barely afloat. Water passed right through it, in the sides and out the bottom, and the bits of flotsam floated in the hull like a school of wooden fish.

Then Midgely stood in the wreck, with an oar for a punting pole, and the rest of us pulled and pushed the boat along. It was hard work, but Early Discall laughed and cheered, and I was pleased to see that his fall had knocked away none of his humor. To himself he hummed the plowman's song he'd sung before.

When the boat was hauled up at the place called Sheerness, we rolled it upside down. Then Mr. Mullock asked Midgely to "hassist 'im." He said, "You can fetch and carry from the caves."

I longed to see his caves myself, so volunteered to take Midgely's place. "He can't see," I said.

"That's true," said Mr. Mullock. "The darkness won't bother 'im, then. Hah! You'd be 'alf off your nut from staring hat nothing. But it won't bother young Midgely."

If there was one thing I'd learned of Mr. Mullock, it was that nothing could be gained by arguing. So I watched him go with Midgely, up through his fanciful city and into the cave. They must have been gone an hour or more, and when they came out it was as though they had been to a chandler's.

They carried nails and bits of bent wood, an oar and a new tiller. Between them, on their shoulders, they bore a short mast with a red sail bundled along its length. These, said Mr. Mullock, were all that remained of his own ship. But that didn't quite make sense to me. "All this comes from one boat," I said. "Like a longboat, not a whole ship."

"Well, 'ow do you think I got to shore?" he asked. "The ship went down; I got in a boat. What could be simpler than that, you chowderhead?"

"What happened to everyone else in the ship?" asked Midgely.

"It's a sorrowful tale, I tell you. They're gone, lads," said Mr. Mullock. "Drowned like rats, every blessed one from the captain to the cabin boy."

"But this is all you saved?" I asked. "Bits of a *boat*? What happened to the ship itself? What happened to the cargo?"

Mr. Mullock had been pleasant enough until then. Suddenly his eyes were blazing with fury. "Don't you dare question me," he said. "I'd hadvise that very strongly."

"It's not that I doubt you," I said. "I just—"

"You don't know why you're 'ere, do you, lad?" he cried. "You 'aven't the slightest idea what Fate has in store for you. Well, I do. Hah!" He bobbed his head up and down, and the bat swung in his hair like a brown bell. "There's a terrible day in the hoffing. A terrible, terrible day."

The bat began to twitter and shriek, as though in the greatest fear. Mr. Mullock patted the little creature. "No, Foxy, that's over. There'll be no more; I've told you."

"What do you mean by that?" I asked. But Mr. Mullock only turned away. I raised my voice and said, "tell me *what*? I want to know."

"What you want and what you get, it's never the same, now, is it?" He chuckled, then went straight to work on the longboat. Or, rather, he stood with his hands on his hips and wondered where to start. He walked around the hull. Half-heartedly, he pulled at a loose nail, then looked up. " 'Ave any of you, by chance, happrenticed to shipwrights?"

We shook our heads. "Midgely grew up in a dockyard," I said.

"But I never built no boats," said Midge. "I never even drove no nail."

"I might 'ave guessed," said Mr. Mullock.

"But you know who has?" asked Midge. He looked toward each of us with his blind gray eyes. "Benjamin Penny, that's who."

"Penny built boats?" I asked.

"Hardly!" scoffed Midge. "It was coffins, Tom. He used to talk on the hulk about his master, what made coffins."

"Hah!" shouted Mr. Mullock. "You brought a coffin maker to my island, did you? There's Fate at work for you." Behind his beard, his skin looked pale. "Tom, you run and bring 'im 'ere."

"No, don't!" cried Midge. "Please, Mr. Mullock, I don't want him here. He's the one what blinded me, Mr. Mullock."

"Is 'e?" Mr. Mullock touched Midgely on the shoulder. "Well, lad, 'ow about this: an eye for an eye? 'Ow does that sound to you?"

His words struck me cold. But the small smile that came with them was worse.

"Crikey, I couldn't blind him," said Midge. "I'm a meek now, Mr. Mullock. Ask Tom if I ain't."

"A meek, are you?" said he. "Out to inherit the earth, I suppose."

"Yes, sir." Midge nodded. It was just what I'd taught him in the prison hulk.

"Now, if I was you," said Mr. Mullock, "I'd let this Penny

do the work. I'd sit right 'ere and watch 'im. And then, when 'e was done, I'd launch the boat and leave the boy behind, that's what I would do. Leave 'im blind to the world for hevermore. That's what I call justice."

Surprisingly, Midgely agreed to that. Mr. Mullock clapped him on the shoulder and sent me off to find Benjamin Penny.

———

eight
I HEAR A DEAD MAN'S TALE

I saw Gaskin Boggis first, as I trotted up toward the summit. He was standing near the top, the tallest thing on the island. Weedle and Carrots and Benjamin Penny were kneeling on the ground, playing slide-thrift with pebbles.

I scuffed my feet, and they all turned as one to look.

"Why, it's Tom," said Gaskin. He waved to me, and called out a greeting.

Weedle told him to shut up. "No talking with the enemy."

I took a few more steps, then stood below them on the trail. Gaskin looked like a statue looming against the sky.

"What do you want?" said Weedle. "It ain't water, we know that. You got water and you got oil; we seen it. We seen that green man too."

"I've come for Benjamin Penny," I said.

"What for?" asked Penny.

"You made coffins once. You can help us fix the long-boat."

"Wal-ker!" said Weedle. "He won't do nothing for you."

He was his old self now, again the king with his court around him. Carrots sat grinning, his red hair dusted to white. I guessed he'd been scrabbling in the dirt to find food for Weedle.

"Now hop it!" Weedle picked up a stone from the ground.

"Without the boat you're stranded," I said. "We're all marooned without it."

"No, we ain't," said Gaskin. "There's people coming, Tom."

He pointed north, but I couldn't see beyond the summit. Weedle hurled his rock at me. "Go on!" he shouted again.

I turned and jogged across the slope, skirting the hill. I came to a ridge that looked to the north, and saw a feather of grey smoke rising from the nearest of the distant islands.

I was to wish later, with all my heart, that the smoke had been the only thing I saw that day. But Mr. Mullock's island sprawled below me, and I found myself looking straight down at the neck that divided it in two. Spanning that space was the pile of stones I'd spotted from the longboat. From there it had looked like a jumbled mass thrown together by winds and waves, or tremors in the Earth. But now I saw that the stones had been carefully placed, one wedging another, as cleverly as any mason could have managed. I knew right away that I was looking at Mr. Mullock's wall, and of course his warnings of the Gypsy were the next thoughts in my mind. I found that in that lonely place, with the great heap of stones before me, it was suddenly not so easy to laugh at those warnings. I decided that I didn't really care what lay beyond the wall.

But as I turned away, I saw that it was steepest on the side away from me. Mr. Mullock had never made that wall to keep out Gypsies. It had been built by someone else. To keep out Mr. Mullock.

I took a few steps from stone to stone, climbing halfway up the rubble. I thought I might satisfy myself by going just high enough to peer across the top. I saw that the island was much the same on the other side. The rocks were just as white, the ground just as barren. There was no movement, except from a cluster of birds pecking away in a cleft of rock.

But why were they there? It seemed strange that birds on one side of the wall left the island to feed at sea, and those on the other stayed behind. I wondered what it was that made them peck and squabble, that sent swirls of them suddenly circling through the air.

I wanted to hurry and tell the others of the smoke in the distance. I wanted Midgely, especially, to know that people were coming. But I thought I might not have another chance to cross the wall. For a moment I dithered. Then I decided it would take only a few moments to run to the birds and back.

Up to the top and over I scrambled. I went not at a run after all, but at a cautious walk. I sent the birds into flight. And I found a man below them.

He was lying in a small ravine. Swarthy of skin, black of hair, he did indeed seem Gypsy. He was wilder than Mr. Mullock, a man in utter rags, shoeless and filthy. I knew at once that this was the running man I had seen.

But never again would he run. His skull had been caved in at the front, perhaps by a fall, but just as easily by a blow from an axe. The skin on his forehead was split, and tiny bits of sand and shells were stuck to the tattered edges of the wound. His hands, his face were bird-pecked, and he lay at my feet with his life pouring from him.

I clambered down into the ravine. I stooped beside him, reached out to touch him. And suddenly he moved.

His eyes flew open. His hand reached up and grabbed my arm. "Kill him," he said in a whisper. "Kill him quick before he kills you all."

"Who?" I asked foolishly. "Mr. Mullock, you mean?"

With a rattling moan, he took hold of me with his other hand as well. "We were seven in number," said he. "But he done for us all. He done for us each in turn."

"Why?" I asked.

But he'd spoken his last words. His eyes rolled up and, with a tremble, he was gone.

His eyes remained open, his teeth in a terrible smile. I had to pry his fingers from my arm, fearing all the time that Mr. Mullock would suddenly appear above, come to find where I had gone. I fled from the place and over the wall.

As Boggis had said, the island seemed haunted. It rang with the cries of murdered men. I imagined that I was racing over their hidden graves, and I heard them shout; I saw the ground shift as they struggled up from below. I ran and ran, and didn't look back until I reached the streets of the tiny city.

I slowed then. I gathered myself, wondering what to do. Things made sense now that hadn't before, and Mr. Mullock suddenly seemed like a monster. "That's over," he'd kept telling his little bat, and he must have meant the killings. But what was I to do: challenge him outright? Pretend I'd seen nothing?

I leaned against the high wall of the Admiralty, still breathing hard and fast. The face of the dying Gypsy hovered in my mind, and I still felt the grasp of his fingers.

Behind me, pebbles crunched. Every muscle in my body seemed to leap and tighten. Mr. Mullock called out, "Did you see 'im?"

I was about to lie, to tell him I'd seen no one. But my voice caught in my throat, and Mr. Mullock strode up the Mall.

" 'Ave you gone deaf now?" he asked. "I said, did you see that boy?"

"Penny?" I said, my voice a squeak. "Yes, I saw him. He won't come and help."

Mr. Mullock looked into my face. "You're white as a sheet. What else did you see?"

"Smoke," I said quickly. "On one of the islands there's smoke. The others won't help because people are coming."

"The junglies!" said Mr. Mullock. He suddenly looked as fearful as I felt. He clawed at my arm. "Are they coming now? Did you see the boats?"

"Only smoke," I said.

"Then there's time," said he. "There's still time, thank God."

He pulled me down to the beach. From the top of the slope he shouted at Early and Midge, yelling as he ran. "It's the junglies!"

I hadn't known until then that fear could spread like a plague. Not I nor Midge nor Early had the slightest idea what a junglie was. But I saw the blood leave Midgely's face, and drain as well from Early's, and suddenly I feared junglies more than I'd feared anything in my life, including Mr. Mullock. I couldn't stand in terror of a man who was terrified himself.

"Hurry!" he cried. "It's our lives now, lads."

We took up the wood; we took up the nails; we swarmed across the longboat. It was as though we, like Noah, had been instantly given the knowledge of shipwrights. I threw a plank atop the hull. Early laid down another, and Mr. Mullock whipped out his axe, all ready to hammer. But that was as far as we got.

We weren't shipwrights; we weren't Noahs. We didn't know even how to start.

"Patch 'er up," said Mr. Mullock. "Cover the 'oles with patches; that'll do us."

"They'll only come loose again," I said. "The boat will sink."

"If we're not off the island we're lost," said Mr. Mullock. "We 'aven't a chance. Not a 'ope."

Then Midgely piped up. "How hard can it be?" he asked. "There's proper idiots building ships, you know. Men with two saws and no thumbs." He parted his hands in a shrug. "We can do it if we keep our heads."

Mr. Mullock cackled. "You 'ear that, Foxy?" He cuffed his bat, and it shrieked. "That's the ticket, lad; keep our 'eads!"

"What do you mean?" I asked.

"The junglies," said he. "They 'unt for 'eads."

My spine tingled. Headhunters. The first of my father's dangers.

"But wait," said Mr. Mullock "They might not come, I suppose. Why should they, to a place like this? They don't know that hanyone's 'ere."

Then Early said, as casually as anything, "Oh, I think *that* might tip them off."

He was looking inland. He was nodding. "Yes, I think they're bound to see that."

From the mouth of Mr. Mullock's cave swirled billows of smoke. It was black and greasy, bubbling up like tar. Yellow flames danced on the rock, and out from the cave came Weedle. He was staggering backward, dragging a ball of fire.

"My oil!" cried Mr. Mullock. "They've lit my bags of oil!"

nine

I EXPLORE THE CAVES

Behind Weedle came Carrots. They each had a sack of oil, and they hauled them together across the ledge. Together they rolled them over the cliff.

The bags tumbled down, spewing fire and smoke. They burst upon London, and the fiery oil flowed into the Thames. It spread to the south, under the bridges and past the Tower, racing to the sea. The smoke went higher and higher.

Mr. Mullock howled like an animal. He brandished his axe, and he shouted at me. "This is your doing, isn't it? Look what you've done!"

"I did nothing," I said.

Mr. Mullock turned as purple as a plum. "You came to my island!" he roared, and raised his hand and knocked me down. He lifted his axe again, and I thought he was going to cleave me in two. The blade hung high above his head, sparkling with the flames and sunlight. Then it came flashing down. But it flew from his hand and clattered across the rock; he had hurled it away in his fury.

"Go!" he shouted. "You cabbagehead! Try and save what oil is left!"

He kicked me as I got up. He pushed me forward. I went up the slope as fast as I could, and Weedle and Carrots fled as I climbed. Mr. Mullock and Early—and even Midgely—frantically stomped at the fire.

The cave was full of smoke, and all across the floor, the bags of oil were burning. They lay like flattened sausages, raging in flames from end to end. Oil was still spreading from them, flowing through the cave and down to the chambers.

I took a breath and dashed to the far wall, straight to the back where Mr. Mullock kept the bags. But Weedle had thrown them here and there, and only one could I see. It lay in the next chamber, beyond a narrow passage. On hands and knees I crawled toward it, surprised to find that the smoke was not as thick near the ground. I could breathe there, though the heat and smoke smarted in my lungs.

I came into a room not much bigger than the maintop on my father's ship. I could span the floor with my arms, and saw that it dropped straightaway to a third chamber some six feet below. A trickle of burning oil had reached the edge and was now falling—drop by drop—to that lower place. Little beads of fire sizzled through the air, bursting at the bottom.

I looked over the edge and gasped. Five faces were staring up at me.

71

From the depths of the cave rose a shriek. It was shrill and deafening, a terrible scream that came amid a fluttering din, as though a hundred carpets were being beaten of dust. Then a dark wall rushed toward me.

I thought it was smoke, but it was bats. By the score and by the thousand they flitted past, all twittering and crying, bouncing from the walls, from my shoulders and my head. My face to the ground, I looked down at a row of skeletons lying side by side. The bones of their arms were stretched out, their fingers splayed. In the flickering shadows, the skeletons seemed to shift and roll like five in a bed, trying to find comfort on the rocks.

I grabbed the bag of oil and hoisted it up. I toppled it into the higher room and clambered after as the bats swarmed around me. From above came a burst of flames, a blast of air, and the flow of fire quickened.

Passages that I hadn't seen before suddenly opened on every side. I saw a pile of metal that I knew at once to be a heap of convict irons. I saw the clasps, the chains and heavy balls. Nearby was a mound of black cloth, and beside it lay a hat—the sort of low-crowned one worn by a priest.

The smoke made me cough and retch. If not for the bats I would have lost my way. I picked up the bag and followed them, as though borne along by their wings. I stumbled through the last chamber, then staggered out the door. And I dropped to my knees, spitting up clots of ash.

Mr. Mullock was staring up from the small buildings of his stone city. He called to me to come down, to hurry. "Bring the oil!" he shouted.

My eyes were watery and sore, and tears flowed from

them. With the bag to carry, I couldn't move fast enough to please Mr. Mullock. He came marching up and took it from me.

"It's lucky for you that you didn't come out empty 'anded," he said, giving me his free arm to assist me down to the beach. "This oil's worth more than gold. It's warmth and light; a man can't live without it."

It would forever be a puzzle why he came to help me. To be sure, his first thought was for the oil. But he must have wondered what I'd seen, and I could only guess that it didn't matter to him then. I was still of use to him.

The four of us worked together, patching the holes in the boat. The job we did would have sent a real shipwright stark-raving mad to Bedlam. We covered the hull with scraps of wood, with turtle skin and sinew. Then we rolled the boat over, and tended to broken ribs that bent up like old umbrella wire. Mr. Mullock urged us on, but kept pausing himself to listen, then to ask, "Did you hear that, lads?" He imagined paddles in the surf, drums in the undertow, and chanting voices in the creaks of the longboat's planks.

Each time the sunlight caught his axe I cringed, for I imagined that very blade felling the Gypsy in a cloud of birds, or splitting the skulls that lay in their row in his cave. I worked as hard as he, for I was afraid to look idle. Yet I feared the moment when the work would be done, for then he might find our usefulness at an end.

"I've seen the 'eadhunters once," he said. "Eighty men at eighty paddles in a double-decked canoe. A 'undred warriors in feathers and plumes, and hevery one the most fiercesome thing. Oh, Lord." He hammered faster for a moment, his axe a blur. "Paint on their faces. Bones in their noses. A dozen 'uman 'eads swinging from poles—all 'anging in the breeze like the devil's own coconut shy."

He hammered quickly, then exploded into a blast of oaths, all aimed at me. "You had to come," he said. "You chump of wood. You mallet-headed mullet. Why couldn't you keep away?"

He struck the hull so furiously that he nearly drove the axe right through it. One of our patches popped loose from the bottom, clattering to the stones. He kicked it and swore, but after that he only muttered to his bat, which had taken shelter in the sweaty warmth beneath his shirt.

In the evening the birds came back to the island. In waves that covered the sky, they converged from all directions. Some low to the ground, others high above, they came with their cries and their whistling wings. It was an amazing sight, but only Early Discall stopped to watch it. Bent over the boat, I heard them pass, and felt the air shiver from their flight. The ones we'd displaced with the longboat squawked their way amongst the others, and Mr. Mullock grew angry at the noise.

"Can't 'ear a thing but birds," he said. "What if the junglies are coming now?"

"Perhaps they are," I said, not daring to look him in the eye. I hoped that he would go up to the summit to check himself, and that I might have a chance to tell Midgely what I'd seen. "They might be landing this very minute."

"Hah!" he said. "Why, we've nothing to fear. Dead men tell no tales, but the birds will watch out for us, won't they? If the junglies come, the birds will rise."

We labored into twilight, and toiled as the moon came up. Mr. Mullock set out his lamps, the turtle-shell bowls, and we worked in the glow of the burning oil.

"When we get to sea, first thing we'll 'oist the sail," said Mr. Mullock. "It'll be Midgely in the bow, and the stupid boy to tend the snotter. Tom, you'll 'and the sheet."

I neither knew nor cared what a snotter might be, or what it meant to hand a sheet. But it pleased me to know that Mr. Mullock wasn't thinking of sailing off alone.

"Next thing, lads, we'll run to the east," said he. "A good sea mile or two, that's all. Then we'll lie ahull till the moon goes down, set all sail and steer a long reach to those islands."

This thrilled Midgely to no end. But it wasn't the idea that we'd be going right where he wanted that made him grin in the dark. It was the sudden string of salty phrases. "You're a sailor, aren't you, Mr. Mullock?"

"I'm sure I'd say I am. Ask me quick and I'll tell you so. My young friend, I'm a yachtsman."

"Oooh, a yachtsman," chirped Midgely. "Is that how you fetched up here, Mr. Mullock? Was your own yacht—"

"Hush!" snapped Mr. Mullock. He held up a hand for silence. "Did you 'ear that, lads? You must 'ave 'eard that."

The rustle and mewl of the birds had been a steady whisper all the night. But now it was loud enough to hide the surf's rumble. Something had disturbed them.

We heard stones clatter and click. We whirled around to stare into the darkness.

ten

MR. MULLOCK'S GREATEST FEAR

Out of the night came a quavering voice.

"Hallo?" it asked. "Tom, are you there?"

It was Boggis. He came right up to the longboat with a flurry of birds at his feet. He towered above us all, yet somehow seemed like a small boy. "Tom, you ain't leaving already, are you? Please take me with you. Don't leave me here." He fell to his knees. "It's haunted, Tom. We can hear the dead men crying."

Mr. Mullock cursed him. "You lolloping thick-wit. It's the birds you hear. Pull yourself together."

"It ain't the birds; it's ghosts," said Boggis. "We can hear the dead men rattling in their graves."

"The undertow!" cried Mr. Mullock. I could see by his

face that he'd spent many nights thinking of ghosts, telling himself that the sounds from his cave were only the stones rumbling in the surf. "Don't talk of dead men to me."

"They're calling out," said Boggis. "They're calling to the boat, and the boat's calling back. It's full of spirits here, Tom."

"You can 'ear a boat?" cried Mr. Mullock. "Already you can 'ear it?"

"Plain as day," said Boggis. "The spirits are wailing out there."

"Lads, that's it," said Mr. Mullock. "Launch the boat; we're leaving!"

"It isn't finished," I said.

"Well, we are. Hah! We're all finished, boy, if we're not off this island."

"Take me with you!" pleaded Gaskin. He turned from me to Mr. Mullock. He threw himself at the man's feet and took hold of his ankles. "I beg you."

"Let me go!"

"Please."

"All right," said Mr. Mullock. "All right!"

I believe he would have said anything at all to make Gaskin let go. The moment the boy's arms unwrapped, he stepped away and shouted a string of commands. "Get the water. Get the mast. Get the fish and oil, and for the love of God get the blasted boat afloat."

Poor Boggis must have thought all the commands had been aimed at him. Everything he could find, he snatched up and threw in the boat. The oars and the tiller, the pins and the rudder, the bags of turtle skin and the mast with its sail; all of it went into the longboat. Then Boggis ran to the stern and pulled on the transom.

It had taken four of us to haul the boat up, but Boggis moved it on his own. He tugged and gasped, and tugged again. Then he stopped to catch his breath.

And I heard the junglies coming.

It was indeed a ghostly sound. It was far away, very faint and quiet. There were no words that I could make out, only a chant of many voices, a sound that swelled and fell away like the rolling of the waves. In each hush was a rumbling thump. A thump and a swirl of water.

"What's that?" asked Midgely.

"They beat time with their paddles," said Mr. Mullock. "They never tire; they never stop."

I had no thoughts right then for the skeletons or the Gypsy. I only wanted off the island.

We pushed the boat together, all at once. It skidded down the beach and into the sea stern first. There was a splash and a plume of spray, and the boat was floating. But almost on the instant, a puddle of water appeared in the bottom.

"It leaks," I said.

"Never mind that," said Mr. Mullock. "A boat's like a Cheapstreet strumpet; a few drops and she's tight. Now get aboard, Midgely, and mind you help the stupid one. The lout can row. Tom, you'll push us clear."

"Why me?"

"Blast you, boy!" he shouted. "Do you have to question me at every turn? Would you have the blind boy push instead?"

78

"Golly, I don't mind," said Midgely. "It's nothing to me to get me feet wet, Mr. Mullock."

"You'll sit where you are," said Mr. Mullock. He shoved me aside and got into the boat.

I would never know if he meant to leave me on the island. I suspected then that he did, and later I became almost certain. But at the time it didn't matter, for the birds suddenly lifted in a mass as shadowy figures came running down the hill.

"It's the junglies!" shouted Early.

Out sprang Mr. Mullock. Nimble enough he'd been before, but now he was fast as lightning. "I'll 'elp you, Tom," he shouted.

He on one side, and I on the other, we pushed the boat from the beach. Then we clambered aboard together.

"They're coming," said Early.

But it wasn't the junglies who emerged from the dark. It was Weedle and Penny and Carrots, and they came in a rush. Down to the beach, right to the sea, they stumbled and ran.

"Wait, we're going with you," said Weedle. "It's our boat too, and we got our rights."

I would gladly have left them behind. But Mr. Mullock said, "Bring them in. There's safety in numbers." And seeing that he was at the tiller, and that he had an oar at hand, he had his way, and the three came over the side.

Mr. Mullock fitted the rudder as we crossed the narrow passage. Then we threaded past the rocks and out to sea. Boggis pulled with all his strength. As the heavy oars swept round, the wooden pins they lay against cried out from their sockets.

From the north came the chanting voices, along with the drumming beat of paddles. All but Boggis stared in that direction. "Quiet now," said Mr. Mullock. "Someone wet those blasted pins."

I heard a splash, and the squeals of the oars turned to a wooden rumble. Mr. Mullock certainly knew his way around boats.

But he wasn't much of a carpenter. Before we'd gone a hundred yards I felt water round my feet. A hundred more and it was lapping at my ankles. I said, "I think we're sinking."

Mr. Mullock whipped off his helmet and tossed it forward. "Bail with that, Tom," he said. "Make yourself useful."

I, alone, couldn't keep up with the water. Soon Carrots was bailing, and Early too, each with one of Mr. Mullock's little bowls. Benjamin Penny scooped with his webbed fingers, and our combined effort maintained pace with the sea.

The chanting grew steadily louder, the beat of the paddles more clear and sharp. But stare as we might, the ocean seemed empty all around. Only the tiny moon was visible, so low in the sky that it seemed to float on the sea.

Suddenly it vanished. It disappeared entirely, and as quick as I could blink, there it was again. It pulsed like a star, like a lamp fed by sputtering gas. I couldn't fathom why. No moon I'd seen ever flickered like that.

Then the truth struck me. I was watching a great canoe pass before the moon. Its prow had blotched it out, and now each paddler, passing, hid it for an instant. It flashed and flashed and flashed again. Fifty times it must have gleamed between as many paddlers. I breathed three breaths before the moon turned solid again as the stern went gliding past. It was a canoe as long as a ship.

"Not a sound," said Mr. Mullock in a whisper.

Boggis leaned on his oars, holding the blades high. We stopped our bailing. We sat still, barely breathing. The longboat rose and fell on the gentle swells, and all the stars seemed to swing above us. Our island was now a dark hump, with a line of pale surf at its base. Our world was so quiet that I could hear the drops of seawater falling from the oars. I could hear it seeping through the patches.

But out there, the voices chanted. Out there, the sea split and tumbled as the canoe sliced through it. I saw the wave it tossed up, and the chant came clearly to us.

"Hiiiii-ya, *uhmp!* Hiiiii-ya, *uhmp!*" sang the paddlers.

The first words were high-pitched, the last a deep moan that trembled in the fog. It was followed right after by that rolling drum as the paddles struck the hull.

The canoe took shape in the darkness. It looked like a black beast that thrust its head high, that crawled on a hundred legs. I thought no canoe had ever been built as large as that. Then we saw it more clearly in the moonlight.

The bow soared higher than the height of three men. At its very top was a wooden bird, its wooden wings spread wide, that seemed to fly across the stars. The paddlers, with their strokes and thumps, seemed to give a breath to the beast. They leaned forward as one, and back as one, singing that chant, "Hiiiii-ya, *uhmp!*" Towering above them was a platform of reeds where warriors sat, each in a cap adorned with plumes. The stern was even taller than the bow, a swaying mass of fronds and feathers.

"Hail Mary, mother of God," whispered Mr. Mullock. "Pray for us sinners, now, and at the hour of our death."

I thought it *was* the hour of our death. If the canoe turned, if a single paddler looked to his right, we were doomed.

Already there was half a foot of water in the boat. Mr. Mullock was on his knees, clasping his hands together. I didn't see his bat, but all of a sudden it cried out in that piercing chatter.

"Foxy, hush!" said Mr. Mullock, but the cry went on.

In a flash, he had his hand at his shirt, and he pulled that creature out. I saw it writhing in his fist, one wing flapping loose. Then both of Mr. Mullock's hands were round it. With a twist, and a tiny crack of a sound, he snapped its little neck. He tipped it into the sea, where the bat twitched and trembled, then drew itself into a huddled ball of brown fur.

I heard a breath being drawn, and saw Benjamin Penny shiver in delight, his teeth shining.

Mr. Mullock spared his little friend not another glance, but went back to his whispered prayers. The canoe rushed on toward the island, the paddlers churning the sea to foam. Then the birds took flight as the headhunters swarmed ashore.

"Right, lads. Step the mast," said Mr. Mullock. "Hoist the sail, and lively now if you want to see the dawn."

eleven
EARLY BEGINS TO REMEMBER

It was no easy matter, in the dark, to step a mast and hoist a sail. The boat seemed overcrowded, with Boggis rowing in the middle, and two of us—or more—always busy with the bailers. We pushed and cursed each other.

But we got it done, and the wind came up when the moon went down. Under oar and sail, we steered north.

Mr. Mullock had us shift the weight—so that the boat might sail the better. He crowded Weedle and his lot into the space between Gaskin and the mast. Early Discall and me he put in the bow. Midgely got the place of honor, right at his side by the tiller.

It pained me that he had taken command so clearly. But I remembered Weedle sitting in my very place, whining about who should be captain, and I didn't argue.

83

At dawn, Carrots and Penny were bailing, and we saw the islands close ahead, not in the tidy row I'd thought, but staggered for miles across the sea. It was from the nearest one that we'd seen the smoke; indeed, there was still a thin wisp of gray ghosting up from its trees.

Of the canoe, there was no sign. For all we knew, it might have paddled over the edge of the world. But I didn't care to see Mr. Mullock steering for the smoke.

I said, "You can't land there."

"Just watch," said he. "You'll be surprised what I can do."

Weedle snickered. Penny laughed outright.

"The headhunters will come looking for us," I said.

"No doubt," said Mr. Mullock. "Myself, I'd rather be on land than at sea. If you 'aven't noticed, we're taking on water. I'd like to do proper repairs before we go any distance."

Midgely nodded. "That's right, Tom. It's true enough."

I was stung by that, and by the sudden thought that Midge might turn against me. I rather sulked as the boat sailed on, and I planned to take Midgely aside the moment we landed.

Mr. Mullock steered us into a sheltered cove a mile or two from where the smoke still rose, now thin as a veil. Though he sat in the stern, he was the first ashore, leaping over us all in his hurry. He raced up the sandy beach, overjoyed to see the green of the jungle. Round a tree he capered in his turtle clothes, green himself, like a hairy giant wood sprite.

Early Discall dropped to the sand. He took up handfuls of it, and let it trickle through his fingers. Perhaps he thought he was sifting gold, but it seemed to me that he was *remem-*

bering sand, that a fragment of his life had come back to his mind.

Boggis took it on himself to be the anchor for the boat. He plumped heavily down, holding on to the ragged end of the towline. When Weedle and Carrots and Penny went after Mr. Mullock, I hauled Midgely to a spot at the jungle's edge.

All Midgely cared about, of course, was trying to put a name to the island. He dragged behind, asking a dozen questions: what color was the sand; how large was the island; how tall its peak? "Is the water 'blue as the egg of an English robin'?" he asked, taking a phrase from the reverend's book.

I had no patience then, which must have disappointed him. The water truly was a remarkable blue, but I only grunted and said, "Never mind that." So he stopped, put his hands on his hips, and said, "Well, blast it, Tom, I can't see nothing for myself. Don't you think it's important to know where we are?"

"Oh, all right!" I snapped. We fell into the shade of a tall tree, and I told him what he wanted to know. He listened, and frowned, and said, "We ain't in the book. Not yet."

"Maybe my father's right," I said. "Maybe that book's just nonsense."

"No, Tom," he said. "It ain't nonsense."

I'd put his nose out of joint. He turned his back to me.

As an infant, Midge had known sailors. They'd come to his house every night to visit with his mother—for tea and a chat, he'd believed—and Midge had sat in his parlor with those who waited their turn in the bedroom. He'd heard many stories of ships and the sea, of lands and strange people.

I asked him now, in the uncomfortable silence, "Do you know any tales about convicts, Midge?"

"I might," he said. "Maybe I know lots of them, Tom."

I could smell the smoke from the headhunters' fire. It was the faintest of odors, that disagreeable stench of old ashes. Down at the water, Early was talking with Gaskin. Behind us, the jungle was alive with a chatter of animals and birds.

Midgely couldn't hold a grudge any longer than he could hold his tongue. "I remember the sailors talking about convicts," he said. "They told me about the mutiny on the *Swift,* about the First Fleet and the wreck of the *Guardian* and all."

"Did they tell you about convicts escaping from Australia? Seven convicts," I asked, thinking of the Gypsy.

"Yes and no," said Midge. "There was a rattling good story about convicts in Botany Bay. But I don't know if there was seven men."

I picked a grass stem for myself, and another for Midge. He lay flat in the sand, chewing away.

"Some of the sailors said it was six what got away. One said it was eight, but he was a liar, that one; he was like Carrots. I didn't care for him at all, Tom. But all of the sailors said those men were killers. Not at first, mind; not till they went to Botany Bay. Then they got loose and went up in the hills, and they murdered some settlers there."

"Is that the whole story?" I asked, for he had fallen quiet. At my side he was wriggling in the sand.

"Oh, no," he said. "It's just starting, Tom."

He moved his arms and legs, sweeping out a little nest. "They were caught, those killers. They were all to be hanged.

But—don't you know it?—the night before they was supposed to swing, they killed someone else."

"A priest?" I asked.

"Golly, how did you know?" asked Midge. "Yes, they murdered the priest what came to see them, then they put on his clothes and murdered the guards. Tom, they *throttled* them," he added in a whisper. "Then they escaped in a boat. There was a boat for going out to the ships, and for fishing at the reefs, and they made off in that. Some of the sailors said the sharks got them. The one who said eight got away told how they got home to England and were murdering boys in their beds. But I think he was just trying to scare me, and that's why I didn't like him, Tom."

"What *did* happen to the convicts?" I asked.

He shrugged. "Not one of them has ever been seen since."

"Listen," I said, shuffling closer beside him. "I think Mr. Mullock was one of them."

"Not likely!" cried Midge. "Mr. Mullock ain't no killer."

"The Gypsy said he was."

Midgely's eyebrows arched. "You met the Gypsy? You went over the wall?"

"Yes," I said. I told him about that, and about the caves. I said I'd seen the convict irons and the priestly clothes, and the skeletons in a row.

"I felt them bones, you know," said Midge. "Mr. Mullock, he said they was turtle bones. And you know what else? There was something queer." He frowned. "Mr. Mullock's boat? It was cut in two. Clean down the middle, like a filleted fish. Weren't that a queer thing, Tom?"

"They must have battled over it," I said. "They must have argued something fierce: stay or move on; and move on to where? But it must have been Mr. Mullock who cut up the boat. He was the one with the axe."

"But he ain't no killer. I know he ain't," said Midgely. "We don't know he's in that story. There's men on other islands, you know."

"With convict irons?" I asked. "With priestly robes?"

"I don't know," said Midge. "But if he's a killer, then why's he scared of you?"

"Of *me*? He's not!"

"Oh, yes he is. He is," said Midge, nodding. "Ain't you seen it, Tom? He's scared to death of you."

I laughed. The idea was absurd. But it made me watch more closely, to "keep a weather eye," as my father would have said. And, sure enough, Midge could have been right.

We spent three days on the island, and in all that time Mr. Mullock hardly took his eyes from me. On that first afternoon, after we'd had our rest and our look around, we started work on the boat. Mr. Mullock sent the others off to find branches of the proper shapes, but me he kept nearby—close, but not too close. He was very careful that I never had his axe in my hands, nor even within my reach.

That night, we lit no fire. Though we had the oil—and certainly the means to strike a spark—we sat in darkness, for safety's sake. All day we'd heard the distant rumble of surf, the creak of old trees swaying in the wind, the chatter of the birds. But with the darkness came other sounds—first a faint cry and a shriek. Then something slithered on the ground, and something else crashed in the branches. The jungle was coming awake in a frightening chorus.

I and all the boys were city bred, and those sounds we'd never heard. There was an unearthly whine that rose and fell, that sometimes hummed and crackled. Worst of all were the bloodcurdling screams that came now and then, or a howl that set my hair on end. With every creak and snap of wood, someone said, "What's that, Mr. Mullock?"

He gave us all sorts of answers. "Parrots," he said at one sound. "Monkeys" at another. Of the whine he said, "Bugs." Always he answered with only one word. But finally, and suddenly, he roared out at the top of his voice, "Shut up! For the love of God will you all shut up! I don't know what's out there! It's junglies; isn't that enough?"

He was terrified. He was the most frightened of any, by far, and his outburst shocked the jungle into silence. Then, slowly, the sounds returned—the whine, the snaps and the screams. It grew so dark that we couldn't see each other, though we sat in a tight little group.

And then—for no reason at all, it seemed—there was utter silence all around, the stillness of a graveyard. In a sense it was more alarming than the noise. But it wasn't really the quiet of the jungle that made my heart beat a fast rattle in my chest. I found that Mr. Mullock had shifted round, and now was right behind me. In the first moment of that quiet, before it struck him that the noise had stopped, I heard what he'd been muttering all the time. "Pray for us sinners," he whispered.

I didn't think much of it then. I was too busy listening to the quiet. No one spoke a word, but all of us knew that the jungle was silent because something was passing through it. We all must have imagined our own horror. For me, it was a line of headhunters creeping toward us, parting the bushes, and staring out with eyes that could somehow see through the blackness.

My every nerve and muscle quivered. I felt that I might scream.

Then Early Discall laughed. "Gosh it's quiet, ain't it?" he said. "Minute ago it's fair duddering; it's a beehive out there, and now it's quiet as me granfer. She never spoke a word from Christmas to Christmas."

"What's a granfer?" asked Boggis.

"His grandma, he means," said Carrots.

"Oh, it's clear and sheer quiet right enough," said Early. He went on, in his old way, about just how quiet it was, and no one minded at all. His voice was soothing. It filled an awful gap until the jungle again began to ring with all its sounds. Then his voice faded away, and we went back to our fearful listening. No one slept until the first gray of morning came to the sky. Then everyone did, except Mr. Mullock and me. We both stretched out on the sand with the others, but on opposite sides of the little group, and every time I looked at him, he was looking back at me.

The days that followed were all alike. We stopped working on the boat as darkness fell, then huddled until dawn. Early chattered away, for he was beginning to remember things from his past, and was becoming again the cheery fellow who had kept us from each others' throats. I caught Mr. Mullock smiling at the odd west-country words that tumbled from the boy's lips.

But we were far from a contented, happy lot. There were many oaths cast in all directions, and much secrecy among the little groups we formed. I would see Weedle conferring with Penny, or Mr. Mullock with Carrots, and worried anew that Midgely and I might be marooned by the others. Benjamin Penny found his fun in taunting Boggis, and at times we all detested one another. Then Early would burst out with one of his silly chatterings, and for a time we'd be at peace.

But as it turned out, he might have done better to keep quiet.

twelve

A DIFFERENCE OF OPINION

We repaired the boat as well as we could in a place such as that. Mr. Mullock showed Gaskin how to split new planks; he taught Weedle and Carrots how to fashion knees from the crooks of branches. He did precious little of the work himself, but it wouldn't have been done without him.

At noon on our ninth day, we launched the boat. Mr. Mullock was back in his place at the stern, and I at mine in the bow. We set the red sail and went flying to the north.

The longboat now looked like something made by trolls or elfin creatures. It bristled with branches and twigs and leaves. But it carried us well, and didn't leak more than a pint every hour.

We passed in short order through the scattered islands,

for the wind blew fresh and steady. Mr. Mullock proved himself very much the sailor, though not a very gentle one.

As I was in the bow, I had to work the snotter. It was a short leash that held the foot of the sail to the mast, and when the wind was against us—as it was in the islands—it had to be freed and tightened each time the boat came about, so that the sail could be set on either side of the mast. But I knew nothing of that in the beginning.

"Tend the snotter!" Mr. Mullock shouted at me the first time we tacked. "You dotty crock, cast off the snotter!"

The sail was shaking. The mast trembled, and I thought the boat would surely founder.

"Hurry up, you sheep's head!" bellowed Mr. Mullock.

It was Midgely who saved me. "It doesn't help to shout," he said. "Tom's the son of a sailor, you know." To which Mr. Mullock replied that I was certainly the son of something.

Midge felt around the mast and found that bit of rope. Then he explained its workings and its purpose, and after that I had no trouble. "I think you might have told me that yourself, Mr. Mullock," I said.

He glared at me. "If I want your hopinion, I'll ask."

Under his hand, the longboat lifted on the waves and raced across the sea. From crest to crest it bounded, flinging spray in glittering clouds. Midgely's face lit up with a broad smile. He said, "You're a cracker sailor, aren't you Mr. Mullock?"

"I'm sure I'd say I was," said he, with the smuggest of looks. He flashed a quick grin through his wind-torn beard.

I'd had enough of him. "What else would you say that you were?" I asked.

The grin fell away. But he said nothing.

We sailed ever north, through the day and through the night. We passed islands so tall that their peaks were covered in clouds, and others that were nothing more than a single tree rooted in a scrap of rock or sand. We passed islands that weren't even islands—only heavy surf and the smell of land, where the rocks didn't rise beyond the surface.

I had to describe each and every one to Midge, who sadly shook his head and pronounced, "We ain't in the book yet, Tom." More and more, I wondered if we would ever find the islands of his book, or the way to the one that we *had* to find.

"I think we have to go east," Midgely decided at last. "Mr. Mullock, could you steer a point to the east, please?"

"No," said Mr. Mullock simply.

"But it's the way to the book," said Midge.

"The book, the book," said Mr. Mullock. "I'm sick to death of 'earing about that hinfernal book. We need only go north and we'll fetch Shanghai."

No one had spoken before of going to any place but Midgely's elephant island. Now the idea was there, and Weedle was quick to side with Mr. Mullock. So did Penny, and then Carrots, who'd always claimed to know everything, and now of Shanghai as well. "My uncle went there," he said. "He met the king of Shanghai in the palace. They were going to make him a prince but—"

"You don't even know where it is," I said. "None of you do." I was the only one who had studied geography, but I couldn't have placed Shanghai on the globe to save my life.

"You muggins," said Mr. Mullock. "We'll 'ave all the ships from all the world to guide us when we're close."

"Yes, even the navy," I said. "Will you hail a frigate and ask directions, Mr. Mullock?"

"Hah! You young spark, if I was any closer I'd give you a twitcher," said he. "What do you expect to find to the east but cannibal islands?"

I stared back down the length of the boat. "The way home."

He let out a vile oath. But Boggis turned and looked at me, and with sad longing said, "Oh, I'd like to go home."

"You're as dotty as 'im," said Mr. Mullock. He looked up at the sail, then pushed the tiller and took a turn on the sheet. "You can't *ever* go 'ome, you miserable muggins. I'll tell you, it's irons and chains that wait for you there. They'll be on you before you know it, and you'll wear them on the treadmill, and you'll wear them in the sweatbox. You'll still be wearing chains the day you go rattling to your grave."

He put a fright into Weedle with that, and worse into Benjamin Penny. "Try to take me home and I'll kill you," said Penny, glaring at me.

Boggis sighed. "I want to go where Tom goes," he said, which pleased me greatly.

I stood up, I held on to the mast as the boat reeled across the waves. "Listen," I said. "It's thousands of miles to Shanghai."

Mr. Mullock blanched. "It's not," he said. "But what if it were? It's 'eaven on earth, that's Shanghai. No questions asked. You're pipe-merry the day long, and at night you're doing the handie-dandie with the most beautiful women in the world—not that you'd care for that now, but you will."

"Let's go to Shanghai!" cried Carrots.

Mr. Mullock stood up. His clothes of turtle skin rippled in the wind, but his clotted hair lay stiff on his shoulders. "Well, it's settled then," said he. "Shanghai it is. If anyone says hotherwise, we'll pitch him over the side."

"Do it now!" cried Weedle. His scar pulsed.

"Pitch them over!" shouted Penny.

We had never been so close to fists and fury. It would surely have come to that a moment later if not for Early Discall.

"What a diddlecome lot," he said with a laugh. "You'd think you've all got the bellyharm, the way you carry on. East or north, what's the difference when you don't know where you are? You've gone and given each other the flickets, and all for what?"

He flapped his arms, then—having said his piece—smiled around the boat.

No one cared what Early thought. His words had not the slightest effect. But I, like everyone, looked at him. They stared at his front, and I at his back, so they didn't see what was just then appearing on the horizon.

"Look," I said, raising my arm.

Mr. Mullock thought I was pointing to him. "No, *you* look," he said. "I knew from the start, from the moment I saw you, that—"

"Look!" I shouted. "It's the headhunters."

The canoe was coming "hull up," as a sailor would have said. The tall fronds at its stern swayed on the skyline, and the black of the hull was a dot below them. I might have thought it was an island—a small island with trees in the wind—if not for the bright colors of those plumes.

Our squabble was forgotten. Whatever Mr. Mullock was about to tell me, whatever he'd known at our meeting, went unsaid. He saw the canoe, then tightened the sheet and pushed the tiller, and sent us rocketing through the waves.

There was an island a league to our left, and a pair of others on our right, some greater distance off. It was toward those that he steered, for that was the way the wind was blowing.

"They won't 'ave seen us," he said. "It's only blind chance that's put them in our wake. Hah! They 'ave the brains of peas, those junglies."

Our longboat bucked and tossed. It reared up on the waves and hurdled the crests, then fell into streamers of spray. It rolled; it groaned, and the rudder shook in its pintles with a sound like chattering teeth. But the canoe came faster.

Steady as a rock, it rose from the water. It grew bigger and blacker. We saw flashes of color from the feathers of the warriors, and then the paddlers below them. I felt it would keep coming like that forever and ever, that nothing could stop it.

It was too frightening to watch. I stared instead at the islands, humpbacked and green. They seemed to advance ahead of us at the same speed as the longboat, not drawing any closer until, quite suddenly, they were looming above us. Then the gap opened between them, and I—in the bow— shouted out, "Ships!" I saw a dozen or more, a fleet of fantastic ships. But it was only a cluster of islets, each with a stand of tall-trunked trees. They looked like flat barges mounting ragged sails.

"Where? I don't see no ships," said Weedle.

I sighed. "They're only islands."

Then Midgely sat up. "How many?" he asked.

I couldn't count them. One overlapped the other, and they all seemed to sail along. "At least a dozen. Perhaps a score," I said.

"Is there one like a galleon, Tom?" Midge was peering there himself. The wind took away his voice, so that he had to shout for me to hear him. "An island like a three-master, with a quarterdeck, Tom."

"Why, yes," I said. It was almost as though he could see.

"We're in the book!" he cried. "Tom, we're at the edge of the book."

Midgely turned to me with a huge, triumphant grin. If he'd had eyes he wouldn't have grinned for long, for the canoe had halved the distance between us.

Mr. Mullock trimmed his sail and turned the bow toward the southern island. We scudded into the passage, past the fleet of islets, and rounded up into a tiny cove where a river ran down through the jungle. On either side the trees leaned inward, tangling their branches in the middle. A curtain of leaves and vines hung right to the water, and Mr. Mullock rammed the boat right through it. "Lower the sail!" he shouted.

He cast off the sheet and halyard. We grabbed the canvas and pulled it down, and there we sat among the branches, as nicely hidden as we could be.

"There's a chief and his family what lives on these islands," said Midgely. "The big one's deserted, 'cept for Sunny Wheeler. He's a trader, you know. Pearls and

98

seashells. But if it's a feast you're after, you want to see the chief. His name is Koolamalinga."

"Three cheers for him!" cried Mr. Mullock. "Now shut up, boy. You're talking rubbish."

Poor Midge. He looked shocked, then sad. He couldn't help adding, in the tiniest whisper, "It means Welcoming One." He sniffed and settled back in his place.

The river flowed brown from the jungle, with just enough swiftness to keep the boat pressed against the branches. From all around came the chatter and chirps of creatures. But we heard, in the distance, that too-familiar sound.

"Hiiiii-ya, *uhmp!*"

We didn't move from our spot. We didn't so much as peer out from the branches. I looked at seven faces that seemed much alike—wide eyes turned upward, mouths hanging open. We listened as the canoe came closer, the chant growing louder. We heard the water at its hull, the creak of its steering oar.

"Hiiiii-ya, *uhmp!* Hiiiii-ya, *uhmp!*"

The pace was slow and steady. The paddles beat against the hull with a boom that echoed from the hills. A flight of parrots went flashing up the river. Down with the current came what looked like a log, until it rose in the water, and I saw the yellow eyes of a crocodile. Longer than the boat, it nudged against the planks. It hit softly at first, and then again—harder.

"Oh, crikey," said Mr. Mullock. "It's smelling the turtle skins."

He moved to the center of the boat and kept himself

there, thinking—no doubt—of his own clothes. In a swirl of brown water, the crocodile vanished. We looked to the left and the right but saw nothing. Then we heard a rubbing on the hull, a scraping at the keel below our feet.

Between the branches, I saw the canoe—or glimpses of a thing so big that I couldn't see it all at once. There was a warrior with a necklace of teeth, another with black tattoos on his forehead and chin. There was paddler after paddler, each with huge arms, brown as chestnuts, sweated to a sheen. For an instant I looked eye to eye with a savage whose nose was pierced by a bone, whose ears were stretched around polished shells and dangled halfway to his neck. Then I closed my eyes and waited, and clenched my hands in fists.

The paddlers slowed, and the chant slowed with them. "Hiiii. Ya. *Uhmp!*" they sang, thudding their paddles on the hull. Below us, the crocodile pushed so hard that the boat tipped up. Wood crackled near my feet. There was a rasp as the crocodile passed underneath; then its head surfaced again, its long snout low in the water.

Mr. Mullock looked nearly beside himself. He had brought out his axe and was standing on the stern seat now, gripping the branch of a tree. His green clothes melded with the jungle, and the whites of his eyes gleamed between his helmet and his beard.

The canoe went past. The paddler's chants faded slowly, then quickly hushed as they rounded a point or turned behind an island. Mr. Mullock seized his chance. He grunted and swung his axe, cracking it down on the crocodile's head.

The brown river exploded. A thick, leathery tail lashed across the boat. The crocodile spun over, whirling white and green in the flashes of its belly. Dark blood oozed in the water, and with a terrible silence other crocodiles came slithering from the jungle, down the banks and into the river. They streamed toward us like fat and gruesome snakes, grabbed the beast, and hauled it down. The water leapt and boiled. Whirlpools opened; eddies swirled. We saw the jaws of one creature, the leg of another; then up floated scraps of flesh. Soon all that was left of a thing bigger than the longboat was a shred of scaly skin.

"My, what a lovely place," said Mr. Mullock. "Who's for going ashore?"

No one was. We didn't know if the canoe had gone, or if it had stopped nearby and was waiting for us to emerge. We decided that the island was safer than the sea, and that we would pass the night upon it, and all of the coming day. So we pulled ourselves along the branches, clambered up the riverbank, and hurried into the jungle.

The trees were so huge and dense that I felt like a flea on the back of a dog. We spent the better part of an hour bashing through the first few yards. Then the jungle opened into glades and meadows, and we came to the foot of a low mountain. A stream fell down in strands of silver, into a pool that was clear and deep. It was there we chose to stay.

And it was on this island that one of us met his end.

thirteen
A MOST UNFORTUNATE CHAPTER

It was Mr. Mullock's idea that we keep a lookout. "Turn and turn about," he said. "We'll go in horder of our age, starting with the youngest; that seems the fairest."

Well, to him it was. He stretched out on the rock beside the pool, like a green lizard sunning itself. He had hours to wait until his turn, if that ever came around. Midgely was the youngest. "Off you go," said Mr. Mullock to him, barely raising an arm from the ground. "Over there is best, I think. Up on that ledge, away from the sound of the falls."

"But he can't see," I said.

"No matter. You never see the junglies anyway," said Mr. Mullock. "But the boy's got ears, 'asn't 'e? Can't 'e listen as well as you or I?"

"It's all right. I don't mind to take my turn," said Midgely.

But I couldn't let him sit alone at the edge of the jungle. "We'll share each other's watches," I told him. "It will make the time go faster."

That may have been what Mr. Mullock wanted all along, for he called Weedle to his side as soon as Midge and I went off across the glade. What was said between them, I would never know.

We climbed to the ledge and found it bathed in sunlight, but cool from the mist of the falls, a pleasant place to sit, if it had not been for the dangers that kept us on guard. We talked little, for there was little to be said after the first few moments. Midgely liked and trusted Mr. Mullock, and refused to hear ill of him.

I fashioned a rough sort of sundial from a twig and a handful of pebbles. I watched our time pass in the swinging of a shadow; then down we went and Carrots took our place. He was followed by Benjamin Penny, and Penny by Weedle, and so the day passed into evening. And then we learned that the island wasn't quite as empty as Midgely had thought.

From a distance, we heard drumming.

It was not the sound of the headhunters' paddles, but a faster and wilder rhythm, a rattle inside of a thunder that must have come from fifty drums or more.

"Where's that coming from?" asked Midge. "There ain't a village for a hundred miles."

"So much for your *book,*" said Mr. Mullock. "You prattling blind boy."

"But it's true," said Midge. "We seen the fleet of islands, didn't we? The galleon and all." He frowned, then smiled and said, "Here, I know, Tom. There's Indians come from all over to visit Koolamalinga. That must be right; it's a gathering."

"Oh, it's a gathering all right," said Mr. Mullock. "They're cannibals, you fool. Listen to the drums. That's a cannibal feast beginning."

With the darkness came a glow of fires in the east, and voices along with the drums. They weren't much louder than the insects that clicked and hummed and whirred around us. But it was frightful to sit there listening, so our tattered group huddled closer together as the jungle also came alive with shrills and shrieks. The last lookout had come down from the ledge at dusk.

The water from the falls burbled and splashed. In its mist rose the moon, a silver ring above us. I could see Benjamin Penny pressed against the rock, as ugly as a gargoyle. He stared straight ahead, starting at the cries of the animals, and that dreadful drumming went on.

Even Gaskin Boggis looked scared. There was a tremble in his voice when he turned to Mr. Mullock and asked, "Will you tell us a story?"

"No," answered Mr. Mullock.

Then Early Discall began to hum his plowing song. He held his arms around his knees and, rocking on the stone, hummed it loud and clear. What a relief it was to hear him. The song was lovely, like a hymn, and it echoed from the rocks and trees and drowned the sounds of drums. He reached the point where a man would answer, if he were really singing in the fields. And suddenly, into his song, came the deeper voice of Mr. Mullock.

He put words to the tune, and seemed to do it without thinking, for he sat as sullen as the rest of us.

Suddenly Early stopped. "Why, you're a plowman," he said.

"What?" said Mr. Mullock. "What are you blathering about now, you simpleton?"

But even Weedle understood. "You was singing his song," said he. "You're from the west country, ain't you? You're from the same place as 'im, Mr. Mullock."

"Don't talk such rot," said Mr. Mullock. "I'm a lord, haren't I? Hah! Do you see lords plowing fields, you miserable—"

"Here, I *knew* a Mullock," said Early Discall. "Why, it was thick with Mullocks where I was."

"Well, I don't know them," said Mr. Mullock. "And furthermore, I don't care to listen to your prattle."

"There was a Mullock three fields over from us," said Early.

Mr. Mullock roared at him. "Are you deaf? Lord almighty, I wish that *I* was."

"Yes, I remember now." Early was scratching his head. "There was a story of a Mullock what went away to London. He—"

"Shut up, you pile of muck." Mr. Mullock leapt to his feet. Three paces he took toward the boy, then three paces back. He whirled around. "Now remember *this*!" he cried. "I've seen things that would curl your teeth, my lad. Hah! I've seen more blood spilt than there's water in the sea. And two things I've learned: no man escapes 'is fate. And dead ones tell no tales."

It was the second time that he'd talked about the silence of dead men. I understood no more about him now than I had the first time. I stared up, as astonished as everyone else, while he stood towering there in his silly turtle helmet, with his great black beard glistening in the moonlight. He pointed at Early.

"You get up on that ledge and don't move until morning. Do you hear me?" he said. "Now!"

Early did as he was told. We watched him slink into the darkness, and heard him scramble up the cliff. A scurry of pebbles came skittering down.

"Now who wanted a story?" said Mr. Mullock. "Well, I'll tell you one, boys. I'll tell you of a fellow who went from rags to riches, and back to rags again. I'll tell you 'ow the world wore 'im down like grain in a grindstone. Is that the one you'd like to 'ear? Is it, then?"

Gaskin blinked back at him. "I'd rather hear about the Mullock what went to London."

"Hah!" Mr. Mullock buried his fist in his beard. He tugged hard, as though trying to wrench the hair from his chin. Then his arm fell to his side and he said, "Oh, what's the use? Am I to be a wet nurse to the lot of you?"

He sat again, in his place. He took his axe from his belt and curled up on his side. The drumming went on in the distance, and the cannibals' fires glowed through the trees like tiny, watchful eyes. Soon a chink and grind of metal started up and I saw that Mr. Mullock was honing his axe on the stone.

"If you've any sense you'll sleep," he said. "It's in the twittering hour that the junglies come."

His blade scraped back and forth. His breaths were heavy sighs. I nodded off, snapped awake, then wouldn't allow myself to sleep again. All through the night, Mr. Mullock ground his axe. At the first sign of dawn he stopped, flicked his thumb across the blade, then stood. His feet straddled Benjamin Penny, who lay more twisted than ever. Midgely was sleeping beside me. I could hear the drums still beating in the east, like a faint heartbeat of the island itself.

Mr. Mullock stepped from the rock to the grass.

"Where are you going?" I asked.

He drew in a short and startled breath. It was the only sign that I'd surprised him. "Up to the cliff," he said, without looking back. "I'll take the morning watch."

I trailed him with my eyes until he passed out of sight around the corner of the cliff. There were no sounds of animals, no cries from the jungle. A heavy stillness seemed to smother the island, and it took a moment for me to realize that the drumming had finally stopped.

The sun came up, a bright slash to the east, and every bird greeted it with a song. It was a cheery chorus that twittered back and forth and all around. I shifted to the side of the pool and took a drink from the clear water. I scooped it to my mouth, splashed another handful on my face, and walked down into the glade.

Up the cliff I looked. Neither Mr. Mullock nor Early was there. The ledge was empty.

My first thought was that Mr. Mullock had gone for the boat. I imagined him racing through the jungle, whipped by branches and vines, hurtling down to the river. I looked all around. I shouted, "Mr. Mullock!"

Then out from the trees came an abominable shriek, and Early Discall cried out, "God save me!" He screamed again. He shouted, "No!"

There came a crashing of branches. "Help!" cried Early. "Oh, God, won't somebody help me?"

On the rocks by the pool, every boy leapt to his feet. Midgely grabbed my arm. "What is it, Tom?" he asked. "What do you see?"

"Nothing," I said. The jungle was a dense wall. A parrot soared up from the midst of it, flapping crazily to the south.

"Is it the junglies?" he asked.

Nobody moved. We could hear poor Early thrashing. He called once more for help, but the plea ended in the most horrible scream. It sent more birds flurrying from the trees.

I saw Benjamin Penny touch his tongue to his lips. His eyes were gleaming bright, his cheeks flushed. He seemed excited, even happy.

Bushes moved at the edge of the glade. The ferns parted, and out came Mr. Mullock. He came at a trot, his hair and his beard streaming back. In one hand he carried his axe, and from the other swung Early Discall's shoes. Halfway across the glade he stopped, threw down the shoes and kicked off his own. "Look lively, lads," he said. "There's not a moment to spare."

"Where's Early?" I said.

"Never mind '*im*." Mr. Mullock knelt to pull on his new shoes. "There's no 'elp now; it's too late."

"You killed him," I said.

"Are you mad?" Mr. Mullock looked from face to face.

"Why would I kill the boy? For his bleeding, blasted *shoes*? Is that what you think?"

"No, not for shoes," said I. "He was starting to remember things. He was coming close to your secrets."

"Hah! What secrets are those?"

"I don't know them all," I said. "But I know about Botany Bay and the priest you murdered there. You've been a busy man with that axe, Mr. Mullock. How many is it now?"

The look he gave me might have melted stone. He came to his feet, encircled now by the boys. I said to them, "He's a convict. He's a killer and a convict, and I say we leave him here."

"Maroon him?" Midgely said.

"Hah! You *are* mad. The whole lot of you," said Mr. Mullock. He was turning in his place, looking to Weedle, to Gaskin, to Carrots, to Midgely. "You're crackers. You're moonstruck. And you're the worst of all, Tom Tin," he said, coming round to me again. "I knew from the start that you were the one. It was you—"

"The priest was the first." I guessed at the truth from what I had seen in the caves. "You chopped the boat in two so no one could leave the island, and you killed the others one by one."

"Did I?" said Mr. Mullock. "Hah! What a tale."

"The Gypsy was the last. But you didn't quite kill him, Mr. Mullock," I said.

There was still a wildness in his eyes. But he managed to gather himself, and took on some of what I thought was the dignity of his imagined lordship. "There's not a word of truth ever came from the Gypsy," he said. "Provising he spoke a word at all to you, that is. I'm of the hopinion that 'e didn't."

"If I want your opinion I'll ask," I said, mocking his words.

He looked as though he might explode with anger. But he kept his voice calm. "If you don't believe me about Early, Tom," he said, "why don't you go and look in the jungle?"

A sound came from there, just then. It was a slither and snap that might have been anything.

"Well?" said Mr. Mullock. "Go and see what 'appened, why don't you?"

I hesitated too long. Weedle laughed. "He's scared," he said.

"As he should be. As he should be," said Mr. Mullock, holding up a hand. "I'll tell you lads, what it was that got your friend. I tried to save 'im, but I couldn't. There were too many."

"Too many what?" asked Midgely.

"Dragons," said Mr. Mullock. "That's what it was, lads. There's dragons out there."

Midgely gasped. "There ain't no dragons, are there?"

"Of course there's not," I said. "Is that the best you can do, Mr. Mullock? *Dragons?*"

"Hah!" He brushed bits of grass from his sleeve. "Off you go then, Tom. Myself, I'm for leaving the island before the junglies come. So what will it be, lads? Who's with me, and who's with Tom?"

I wasn't surprised by the outcome. When Mr. Mullock headed down to the river, down to the waiting boat, everyone but Midgely went with him. Even Midge himself might have gone, if he'd had eyes.

"Oh, Tom," he said. "What do we do?"

There was another slithering sound from the jungle. It seemed to be passing the glade, moving in the same direction that Mr. Mullock had taken. I wanted very badly to see for myself what had happened, but I feared being left behind on the island. I heard in my mind Early's terrible cries and knew that, for whatever reason, Mr. Mullock was right that he wasn't alive any longer. Feeling very much the coward, I told Midgely, "It's true; we can't save him." I took my friend and pulled him away, and together we raced for the boat.

Through the ferns and through the bushes, round the trees we ran. I didn't look back, or to either side. I paused once, to listen for the river, then started off again.

We came to a trail and turned along it. The ground was soft, broken by the footprints of all the boys and Mr. Mullock. Midgley stumbled and fell. I pulled him up. "Hurry," I said, dragging him on.

As we came to a bend in the trail I heard a shout from Mr. Mullock. Branches snapped; he swore and cursed. A moment later we rounded the corner, and I saw with astonishment that he was dangling head down from the trees.

Like a toy man on a string, he swung there, writhing and twisting. A loop of rope encircled his ankles, and his little turtle helmet was rolling on the ground. Curses and oaths poured from his mouth one after the other.

Gaskin Boggis was standing below him. "It snatched him up," he said. "He was running ahead, and all of a sudden he was swinging in the air."

"It's a man trap," I said.

fourteen

DRAGONS IN THE LAND

Midgely snorted. "That ain't no man trap." He was squinting at what must have been a great black shadow dangling above him. "The people here are friendly, Tom. You know that; you read the book."

"Never mind your bloody book," said Mr. Mullock. "Get me down, you loonies."

He was high enough that his reaching hands couldn't quite touch us. They were turning very red, and I imagined his face was the same. But his beard had fallen across it, and he sputtered now to spit the whiskers from his mouth.

"Get me down!" he cried again. "You can't leave me like this."

The thought hadn't really occurred to me. But now that

he'd said it I could imagine doing just that. It would be a pleasure to go on our way without Mr. Mullock.

He kicked in the noose, and set himself swinging so violently that he crashed against a tree. The noose tightened, the rope popping at his ankles. I could see that it was Early's shoes that held him, and that without those his feet might have slipped right through the loop.

"Look," he said. "Please. If you want me to beg, I'll beg. Just don't leave me here for the junglies."

"Tell us the truth," I said. It hurt my neck to look up at him. "You killed Early. Say it's true."

"I didn't," he said. "It was dragons, I told you."

Back and forth he went, a green and hairy bell.

"Say it," I told him.

"Blast you, Tom Tin," said he. "I wish I'd never laid eyes on you. I wish—"

"Come on, Midge." I pulled his arm. "Gaskin, let's go."

"No!" roared Mr. Mullock. "No. Don't go!"

Midgely held back. "Tom, we can't leave him," he said. "Please let him down. The junglies will be here soon."

"But, Midge . . ."

"Please, Tom," he said, so I sighed and said I would.

The rope led up to the branches of a bending tree, then down a side of the trail. Many times it looped around a fallen log and ended in a massive, tangled knot. I called up to Mr. Mullock. "Throw down your axe, and I'll cut you loose."

"Hah!" said he. "Not on your life."

I could hardly believe he'd refuse me. "Well, suit yourself," I said, turning away.

"Wait!" cried Mr. Mullock. "Untie the knot. Or tell that great clumper to break it."

"Don't call me names," said Boggis.

"Oh, never mind him, Gaskin," I said. "We'll leave him where he is."

Mr. Mullock swore. He struggled harder in the noose. He swung the axe wildly, trying to hack himself free, but only spun farther and faster. Then he cried out, and there was fear in his voice. "God almighty, something's coming."

I heard it too. A plodding on the trail, a hissing in the jungle. A massive head appeared between the trees, and a terrible creature stared at us all. It looked like a huge hound made of leather, with lizard's eyes and a mouth full of jagged teeth. Its skin was gray and lumpy, its legs stout—too short—so that its barrel of a chest nearly rested on the ground. Its head swayed side to side; then out from its mouth shot a spurt of fire.

"A dragon!" shouted Gaskin Boggis.

Midgely held me tightly. "Is it true? Is it a dragon?"

"Yes," I said.

"Holy jumping mother of Moses."

It came lumbering closer, rolling as it walked. The ground hollowed beneath its huge, clawed feet.

Mr. Mullock called out from above us. "Here, Tom. Catch it!"

His axe came spinning down. It landed with a thud, its blunt end in the ground, the blade sticking up. At the flashing of light, the dragon's head turned. Another fiery flicker sparked from its mouth.

There was a grunt, or a cough, and behind it came a second dragon, even larger. Like the first it had a long, thick tail, and from end to end it must have measured the height of two men.

I stepped forward for the axe. The heads of both the dragons turned toward me. They hissed; they spat their fire.

Again I moved. And they rushed me.

Their speed was terrifying. Their feet pounded; their long tails lashed in the bushes. In an instant they traveled four yards, then stopped just as suddenly. My heart racing, I stood absolutely still.

I thought one would pounce right then—pounce or roast me in its fiery breath. But both the dragons stood as still as I. Their skin was loose and scaly, their eyes set in bulging sockets on the sides of their heads. I could smell their fetid stench. The nearest hissed again; it blinked.

Above me, the rope creaked around Mr. Mullock's ankles, through the branches, and down its length. The axe and helmet lay at my feet.

"Don't move," I said. "If we stay still they can't see us."

The nearest dragon took one more plodding step. Its legs jutted like buttresses from its shoulders and hips, and I could see the flaps of skin wrinkle and shift. The tiny nostrils puckered. The lips cracked open, and the fire came out.

Then I saw that it wasn't fire at all. It was only a tongue I was seeing, a bright orange tongue that flickered like a snake's.

But Gaskin was farther away. And Gaskin saw fire. He shouted and screamed and turned on his heels. I heard him running down the trail, and the dragons thundered after him. They passed on either side of me, so close a thick tail of one

115

rasped against my knee. One of the beasts planted his foot in Mr. Mullock's helmet and sent it cartwheeling in the air. The other trod right upon the axe, and let out a horrid sort of shriek. With each step, it left a splatter of blood behind it.

I looked back and saw Midgely on the ground. He was curled like a hedgehog, his head in his hands. Slowly, he stood. "Tom?" he asked. "Tom, you ain't eaten, are you?"

I took the axe and chopped the rope. Mr. Mullock tumbled heavily to the ground. The fall thumped the breath right out of him, but he found it again soon enough. He pulled the noose from his ankles, then crawled across the trail and retrieved his little green helmet. He didn't ask for the axe, and I had no mind to give it up.

We could hear the dragons along the trail. There was that quick thumping of their feet, a startled cry from Boggis. And there followed such a furious struggle that the very earth was shaking.

Mr. Mullock, to his credit, didn't hesitate a moment. He darted down the trail, and I—with the axe—took Midgely and went after him. Beyond a bend, and beyond another, we found the two dragons locked in a terrible struggle. They rolled and tumbled, and they slammed against the ground, writhing in a mass of teeth and fire and swinging tails. Beside them stood Gaskin, looking hale and hearty, but scared to death.

"They turned on each other," he said. "One was bleeding and wounded. The other went after it."

So the axe, I supposed, had saved us. Or was it the noose that had snared Mr. Mullock and forced him to give it up? Perhaps it was Early's shoes that had caught the rope. . . . I shook my head. There was no sorting out the little stream of fate. It seemed only that—for once—it had flowed in my favor.

We drew back into the jungle, meaning to circle round the dragons and reach the longboat. But we came instead to the edge of the island, to a cliff above the sea. From there we looked out and I saw that the tide of fate hadn't turned at all.

Out on the ocean, a cable or two from the shore, the longboat was riding on the waves. Carrots was rowing, Weedle was steering, and Benjamin Penny stood in the bow.

Mr. Mullock turned the air blue with his oaths. He leapt up and down with fury. "Come back!" he bellowed. "Come back, you young curs!"

But the longboat rose and fell on the waves, and Weedle didn't even turn around. In the height of sauciness, he raised one hand and gave a cheery little wave with his fingers aflutter. I heard Benjamin Penny laugh.

Mr. Mullock nearly exploded. "You blackbeetle boy!" he cried, his face an alarming red. "You'll perish; you all will. The devil take the lot of you!"

Carrots worked his oars at sixes and sevens. He was even worse at rowing than Weedle had been, so bad that he seemed to be doing nothing more than bashing the water with his blades. But the boat kept moving, and soon rounded a point, and the last I saw was Carrot's red head as he stood to ply his oars.

I had never felt so hopeless. I very nearly hurled the axe after the boat.

"This is your doing," said Mr. Mullock. "If you 'adn't delayed me, if you 'adn't hinsisted on getting that axe . . ."

"Then you'd be going with them," I said. "You'd be in that boat right now on your way to Shanghai. And you know, Mr. Mullock, I wish it were so. If I'm to be stranded, I'd rather it wasn't with you."

"Hah!" He turned away to gaze at all the empty ocean.

Midgely was pulling at my arm. "We ain't stranded, Tom. Not really," he said.

"What do you mean?" I asked.

"I keep telling you," he said with annoyance. "Sunny Wheeler, Tom. That trader, he'll help us."

I hadn't really believed in his trader. But he'd said the man was a crocodile trapper, and we'd certainly found a trap. "Where does he live?" I asked.

"Somewhere on the eastern shore," said Midge. "He's got a hut on the beach."

It seemed our only hope, and we all went off to find it, along the trail at first, then downhill through the jungle. I gave the axe to Boggis, who led the way and hacked a tunnel through the bushes. But it was slow going—or perhaps our course was less than straight—and dusk still saw us struggling along. I thought we would have to spend the night in the jungle, but then we heard the cries of seabirds, and just before dark we came out at a sandy beach.

If there was drumming that night we didn't hear it. We had only the birds, and the lap of waves on this lee side of the island, a soft sort of sound like many dogs drinking. We had the moon to light our way, and we plodded north across hard sand.

I carried the axe again, and made sure that Mr. Mullock was in front of me. When he stopped, so did I.

"Tom, look," he said. "This island's too small for 'ard feelings. I'm sorry that Early's gone, but I'm sorrier still that you think I 'ad a 'and in it."

"If you're asking for this," I said, lifting the axe, "you can forget it, Mr. Mullock."

"Farthest thing from my mind." He smiled, in the way that had seemed charming when we'd first met.

"Keep away from me, Mr. Mullock," I said.

"Hah! Count on it, son," said he. "I've said my bit, and it's off my chest."

We walked very far that day. When Midgely tired, I carried him on my back. And when I began to stumble, Boggis said, "I'll take him, Tom. He's so little, it ain't nothing to me."

The shoreline turned toward the east. The jungle above the beach began to thin, and soon there was nothing but bare rock and sand above us. "It's a spit we're on," said Mr. Mullock. "We could cut across here."

"No," said Midge. He'd almost fallen asleep on Gaskin's back, but was now wide awake. "We have to follow the shore all the way. We might go right past Sunny Wheeler if we don't."

For half a mile we trudged toward the moon. It almost seemed that we'd come to a different island, for palm trees took the place of the jungle, and a breeze coming down from the island made their long fronds rustle. Against the stars, they looked to me like giant hands waving at the end of pipe-stem arms.

As we neared the end of the spit, I heard a thud behind us, like a heavy footfall in the sand. When another came soon after, I stopped and looked back. But the moonlit beach was empty, and nothing moved in the black shadows above it. So we carried on, and stopped at the very end of the spit.

"Did you find the hut?" asked Midgely.

I shook my head, but of course he didn't see that. The tip of land stretched into the sea, and one was as empty as the other. Mr. Mullock said it was a goose chase we were on. He sat on the sand, in the moonlight. The breeze gusted; the palm trees swayed. There was another thud, and this time I wasn't the only one to hear it. Mr. Mullock looked around, his beard shining darkly. "Who's there?" he asked.

We held our breaths. I listened to the rustling fronds, to the buzz of flies in the grasses, until my ears rang with the quiet. I peered into the blackness along the shore.

"Oh!" I gasped. "Look."

There was a figure there, leaning on a tree. He was tall and thin, dark as old wood. But he didn't move; he didn't so much as nod, only leaned at a peculiar slant with his arms stiff at his sides. When my heart slowed down I saw that it *was* a wooden man, a carving propped among the trees. The more I looked, the more I saw: three peeled logs planted in a row; a glint of starlight moving; the triangular shape of a roof.

"It's the hut," I said. "Midge, you're right."

"Hah! By George, 'e is," said Mr. Mullock. "Or it's the luck of the devil 'e's got."

We moved toward it, all together. The hut stood on the land, but hung over the beach; the logs were stilts supporting it. The wall was woven grass; the roof was thatched; the glint of light shone from the broken pane of a small window. And a buzzing of flies came out from there.

"Why, it's chock-full of bugs," said Mr. Mullock. "Hah! Poor old Foxy; wouldn't he like to be 'ere?"

It was the first he'd spoken of his little bat, the only sign he'd missed it. In a fashion, it was the first hint that Mr. Mullock had a heart.

We stood below the pilings, beside the wooden man. A furious expression was carved on his face, but a split had opened across the mouth, and now the man looked a lot like Walter Weedle. I touched its cheek, and my fingers came away covered in termites.

"Is the trader here?" asked Midgely.

"Wal-ker!" said Mr. Mullock. "It's as empty as a tomb."

"Then he must be off trading," said Midge. "He paddles from island to island in a little canoe, buying oysters and pearls."

"Maybe he's sleeping," said Boggis.

Mr. Mullock grunted. "Nip in and have a look, Tom. Or give me the axe if you're scared, and I'll go myself."

There was no reason to be frightened; it was only an empty house. But I heard the wind in the palms, and then the footfalls again, the sounds of men who weren't there. I gripped the axe and clambered to the back of the house.

There was a crude ladder leaning against it, a log with steps chopped along its length. It moved when I touched it. When I climbed it, the whole hut trembled and shook, and the drone of flies grew louder.

The door at the top hung open. I stepped into a room that wasn't quite as black as I'd thought it would be. In the small window was the glow of the stars and the moon. In the middle of the floor was a red glint of embers where a fire had collapsed on itself.

I knew then that the hut hadn't been empty for long. I had a strong sensation that it wasn't empty even now.

The air was thick with a musty old smell, a peculiar odor that made me think of old Worms the body snatcher. I heard the flies buzzing around me, and a shiver of wind through the thatching. Then there came such a bang that I nearly bolted from my skin, and down from the roof came a thing—a black thing. It landed on the floor and leapt to the fire. It seemed to burrow into the ashes, and it stirred the embers so that a red light filled the room.

I saw what it was then, this thing that had come at me. The sight made me laugh, for it was only a coconut that had pierced right through the roof, leaving a small oval of stars above me. I knew that all my imagined footfalls on the beach had been only so many coconuts knocked free by the wind.

In the red glow I looked around, into each dark space. I saw a broad shelf above the floor, and what looked like a person sleeping there, but was only a mat rolled into a fat tube. I saw pots and bowls and a heap of wood, a spear propped against a wall. There was a wooden box, a basket and a painted shield, and I kept turning and saw a table in the corner, where a man was sitting in a chair.

His back was toward me. He had fallen forward, so that his chest rested on the table, and all I could see of him was the hump of his shoulders. It was there the flies were gathered—a seething mass of flies that reflected the stars and the firelight in their thousands of flashing wings.

I cried out to him—"Hallo!"—but he neither moved nor answered.

I was certain what I would find, but I still stepped closer. The hut shifted on its stilts, the table creaked, and the man seemed to shrug his shoulders. His right arm had been resting on the table's edge, but now it fell from there and swung back and forth in the space beside the chair. It was a horrible hand, a hacked-away lump reduced to the thumb and one finger.

"Hallo?" I said again. There was still no answer.

I moved forward quickly. I didn't stop until I stood behind him. His other hand lay squarely in the light from the little window. As disfigured as the first, it was a hand with only three fingers and no thumb. I reached out and touched his shoulder, and all the many flies rose up like a great seething boil. They ticked and tapped against me, colliding with my face and arms. There were so many that I was blinded for a moment, and when they cleared away—like a black fog thinning—I saw that the man had no head.

fifteen

THE FATE OF CROC ADAMS

I fled from the house and ran to the beach. In my fear and shock, I could hardly speak. But the others pressed around, asking questions, and I stammered out that I had seen a dead man at a table.

"Do you think it was Sunny Wheeler?" asked Midge.

"He didn't give his name," I said, still shivering.

"But you'd know him," said Midge. "They call him Sunny 'cause his hair's as yellow as the sun."

I heard my own laugh, a crazy sound. "He didn't have any hair. He didn't have any head."

"Oh, Lord!" said Mr. Mullock.

We were all standing on the beach, looking up at the walls and roof of the hut. The flies were buzzing again, and I couldn't get warm, no matter how I held myself. "He had terrible hands," I said. "He had claws for hands."

"He did?" asked Midge. "Like this, you mean?" He curled and twisted his own hands, tucking fingers and thumb out of sight. "Like they was eaten away, Tom?"

"Yes," I said.

"Holy jumping mother of Moses. You know who that is?" Midge gaped up at me. "That's old Croc Adams, ain't it? And don't that explain it all? Croc Adams, he traps the crocodiles and sells them to make purses for ladies. It was a crocodile trap what caught Mr. Mullock."

I couldn't understand Midgely's excitement. "So where's Sunny Wheeler?"

"Gone native," said Mr. Mullock. "Hah! That's what 'appens on these islands. You come out from England and start living the good life, picking your food from the trees. You lie on the beach and swim in the surf, and the next thing you know you're out collecting 'eads."

I wondered if he wasn't describing himself. But then he shrugged and said, "That's what I've 'eard."

"No, no!" cried Midgely. "Sunny Wheeler weren't never here. I thought this was his island, but it ain't. It's old Croc Adams what lives here. And you know what, Tom? *Now* I know where we are."

Mr. Mullock groaned. I said, "Oh, Midge. You keep telling us that, and you're always wrong."

"But I *do* know now," he said. "Them little islands what looked like ships? That galleon island, remember? They weren't what I thought, but I see it now. The reverend called them the Pastry Places, 'cause his daughter said they was like fancy cakes, them little islands. You remember that from the book don't you, Tom?"

"No," I said. Midge had spent years with the book. He'd learned every word. But there wasn't a lot I remembered myself.

"You know where old Croc Adams lives?" said Midgely. "Not five miles from the reverend's mission, that's where he lives, Tom Tin." Midge was nearly shaking with excitement. "It's on that other island. The very next island."

"Then it might as well be on the moon," said Mr. Mullock. "Since we 'aven't a boat anymore."

"You stupids," said Midge. "Don't you think old Croc Adams has a boat?"

He was right, and it was Boggis who found it. We all blundered through the bushes and round about the house, but Boggis went down to the water and found it floating on a mooring. He called out, "Here it is." Then he added, "Least I think it's a boat."

I could see right away why he wondered. It was a canoe that had been hollowed from a log. But it had no front or back; it was more like a trough than a boat. And it was a tiny thing, too. "I've seen bathtubs bigger than that," said Mr. Mullock.

But we piled aboard. Midgely sat in the middle, and I at the back, while Boggis and Mr. Mullock straddled the thing like riders on a little wooden horse. Their shins and their feet were in the water, and they kicked us over the shallows and out to the sea.

We used branches for paddles, as we'd found none of the

real ones, and we rode the canoe from night into dawn, poling and paddling along. There was little talk, for all of us were worried. We were heading for the island where the drums had been beating.

Mr. Mullock wanted to fetch it in the darkness, and kept nagging us to paddle harder. Whenever the water grew shallow, he made Boggis hop out and pull us along. But the sun rose while we still had a mile to go, and we saw the island loom ahead. It was dark and gloomy on the sea.

From its tangled shores, a mountain towered up. A black cliff soared from the jungle in jagged shards and runs of green. It was a most foreboding place, and Mr. Mullock might have been speaking for me when he said, "I'd rather pass it by."

But there was nowhere else to go. The two large islands, and the little islets between, formed a group as lonely as stars in the sky. Miles of sea surrounded them.

"You'll like it when we get there," Midgely said. He was squinting between his fingers, trying to see the place for himself. "The reverend calls it Pig Island, but that ain't its real name. There's no one can say the proper name, it's got so many letters. But it means Place of the Pigs. Them hills is thick with wild pigs."

"Porkers you say?" said Mr. Mullock. "There's porkers running about?"

Midgely nodded. "There's the village, too. A hundred people maybe."

"Hah! Cannibals, you mean."

"No," said Midge. "They're uncommon friendly here."

The thought of all the pork and pigs' feet must have been

too much for Mr. Mullock. He applied himself to his paddle, and the little canoe doubled its speed.

Midgely said he knew exactly where the mission was. He said we could paddle along the shore and land right below it. "The reverend keeps his own boat there," he said. "It's a steamboat, Tom, and won't *that* be splendid? He'll take us straight to the elephant island."

Mr. Mullock said nothing. I saw his back stiffen, though, and wondered what he was thinking. We hadn't talked of where we would go since the day in the longboat when he'd steered north to Shanghai. Now, I imagined, he was only waiting his chance to head there again.

Midgely looked back at me. I saw—for the first time, really—how his skin was blistered by the sun, peeling from his nose and cheeks. But he was smiling away like a boy on a picnic. "We'll paddle right up to the mission, won't we?" he said.

"We'll not do that," said Mullock.

Midgely's face fell. I was about to speak up and say we'd go where we pleased. But Mr. Mullock said, "Look, Midgely. I've taken something of a fancy to you I 'ave. You're a fine boy. But the truth is you're as spoony as they come, and you 'aven't yet been right about that book of yours."

"That's true," said Boggis.

"Where you say there's a mission, as like as not we'll find a cannibal village," said Mr. Mullock. "And, frankly, if we see a single porker I'll be surprised. We'll land right ahead and foot it from there." He raised his voice to be sure that Midgely would hear. "Provising that suits our young Captain Blind."

"Go ahead," said Midge. "Do what you please, and you'll see for yourself."

It was plain to all that he was hurt, though he tried not to show it. He gave me a smile that was comically sad, and said, "What a welcome we'll get, when we get there."

Within the hour we reached the island. We hid the canoe in what looked like a mulberry bush, and went on by foot to the north. We kept the water in sight, though it meant we had to clamber up and down the slopes.

The jungle was thicker than any we had seen. The trees soared up to a solid mass of leaves and branches. Much higher than the masts of my father's ship, they seemed to hold up a whole new world above our own. The small patches of sky were like pools of blue water, in and out of which flashed gaudy birds and mysterious, chattering creatures. I saw a monkey leap across that world, then a huge green frog glide like a bird from tree to tree. I saw snakes that looked like branches, and branches that looked like monsters.

We descended to a gully, then climbed again—and kept climbing—up a slope as steep as stairs. For half a year we had been no higher than a house is tall, and now the air felt thin, the height dizzying. Midgely's nose began to bleed, a redness on his lip.

Boggis kept looking back. "There's someone behind us," he said. "There's savages there."

But we saw no one. Nothing moved except the branches and the ferns we'd passed, closing again to hide our trail. Yet I too became convinced there were savages behind us. It was all the more frightening that I could neither hear nor see them.

We hurried our pace. Over rocks, under fallen trees, we

staggered and stumbled. We followed a stream that ran swiftly at first, then slowed to a brown sludge—as though it, like us, grew weary. We paused more often, looking back as the monkeys hooted and the parrots whistled.

On we went, in spurts and dashes. We waded through mud like molasses, past dangling vines and enormous nests of termites. What seemed at first to be a fallen tree suddenly curled upon itself as we went toward it. It slithered and oozed through the mud, a snake as thick as barrels.

The river twisted amongst the trees. In a long bend it curled from north to south, nearly to its own banks, and we were suddenly looking back where we had been. And there we saw the savages.

Three of them, they came in single file, splashing down the stream. They wore breastplates made of bone and wood, and sashes round their waists. One wore feathers on his head, a waving tuft of scarlet, and all three were draped in strings of shells and bones that hung about their necks. They strode steadily but slowly, as though they had no need to hurry.

"It's all right," said Midge when I told him about them. "They're friendly."

But Boggis snatched him up, and we ran like frightened deer. We hurdled logs; we bounded down the river. But every time we paused—breathless and afraid—we heard the steady sloshing of the savages, and on we went again.

The river flattened near the sea. The ground grew soft and swampy. A buzz and whine of insects grew louder every moment, and didn't that put a fear inside me?

Then we shouldered through a wall of bushes. And there was Midgely's mission.

It sat in a clearing where grass—once cut—now grew wild. The house was wooden, two stories tall, surrounded by a wall of logs set into the earth like pickets. "A mission?" said Mr. Mullock. "Hah! It's a fort." We could see only the roof and a bit of wall, a small window where a red flower grew in a clay pot.

We crossed the clearing quickly. Half hidden in the grass lay a child's pull toy—a big-eared mouse with its bright paint falling away. There was a little pail and a tiny shovel, and a bassinet tipped on its side, full of spiderwebs and brown coccoons.

At the back of the wall was an open gate. It wasn't more than three feet wide, but was so thick and heavy that Boggis and Mr. Mullock had to use all their strength to swing it shut. I threw the bolt to lock it. The clunk of the metal falling into place gave me a terrible sense of unease.

Boggis let Midgely slide from his back, then all of us turned to study the house. It could never have been an inviting place, with its mere slits of windows and its one little door girded in iron. But now it was utterly and hopelessly abandoned. The building, squat and square, was rotting away. The skirting of planks was broken and moldy, the thatched roof wildly overgrown.

"Ain't it splendid?" said Midge. "It's all painted up like a fancy tart, ain't it? Don't the windows sparkle?"

There was something in his voice that made me think he knew the truth but didn't want to admit it. Certainly, he didn't call out for the reverend whom we'd come so far to find. For him, the mission must have been a disappointment that was just too much to face. Not one of us—not even Mr. Mullock—said a single thing to set him straight.

Inside, the house was in mad disarray. Tables and chairs lay on their sides. Heaps of belongings were strewn from wall to wall. I saw books and maps and china cups, an umbrella stand made from an elephant's foot, a broken cello, and a once-fine top hat now crushed like a concertina.

I expected the same upstairs, yet all was neat and tidy there, as though the reverend had left only that morning. There were a large bed and a small one, both carefully made up. Clothing hung in a wardrobe. A candle and a Bible sat on a bedside bureau. I couldn't imagine why the savages—who had clearly sacked the lower floor—hadn't touched this space at all.

I went to the window. I looked out and over the logs, and saw the three savages at the edge of the clearing. Not fifty feet away, they stood mottled by the sunlight and the shadows of leaves. They didn't look at me, nor at anything else, but only stood in their still and quiet row.

Below me, Boggis and Mr. Mullock kept crying out in excitement at all their finds. They uncovered sacks of grain, of beans and flour, then a whole pantry jumbled with horrid-looking cheeses and smoked fish and tins of every delicacy.

"Oysters!" cried Mr. Mullock. "And look! Good heavens, here's tinned ham!"

I searched the wardrobe, hauling out crinolines and trousers and blouses and shirts, until they piled on the floor all around me. I spilt out the bureau drawer by drawer across the bed, but in the whole room I found not a single musket or pistol, nor any weapon of any sort.

I looked once more from the window. Now, where the three savages had stood, a dozen were gathered. In each wall was a window, and on every side of the house I saw more of the savages. In their breastplates, with their spears and bows and blowguns, they stood to the west and the north and the south.

It seemed that we hadn't been stalked through the jungle at all. We'd been *herded,* and now were penned behind the walls like sheep in a slaughtering house.

sixteen
ATTACKED BY HEADHUNTERS

We smelled woodsmoke that afternoon, and in the evening the drumming began. It rumbled through the trees and echoed in the hollow rooms of the mission. Slow at times, and wild at others, it went on without stopping.

On the upper floor, we waited. Midgely slept, and Boggis kept pacing from one window to another. I sat in the middle of the floor, trying to fashion weapons from bedposts and chair legs, splintering their ends with the axe.

Mr. Mullock kept himself busy with a can of cockles. Many times I had watched gulls along the Thames pull cockles from the mud and crack their shells by dropping them from a height. Now Mr. Mullock was trying to split the whole tin, hurling it again and again at the floor. Each time, he fell upon it in a gull's fury, uttering the same shrieks and cries.

134

When the can was squashed and dented, but still whole, he cursed loudly. " 'Ere, Tom," he said. "Give me a go with the axe."

"No," I said.

"Hah!" He cursed me again. "You don't think I'm going to split your skull with it, do you?"

"No, I don't fear you now, Mr. Mullock." I said. "Not when it suits your purpose to keep me alive."

"Lord almighty," he said. "If that's what I wanted, I 'ad my chance. I could 'ave done you in at any time."

"I know very well what you've done," I told him. "I know what I've seen and heard."

"Hah! You think you're such a clever lad, Tom Tin," he said. "It's all your schooling, I suppose. You add things up, and two and two make four to you. But you don't understand the ways of the world."

"Then tell me," I said.

He got up and went to the window. He put his hands on the sill and looked out at the savages there. He talked slowly. "When you first set foot on my island, I knew my end 'ad come. Ah, thought I, 'ere's my angel of death come in the shape of a boy."

I looked at poor Boggis trudging back and forth, at Midgely sleeping beside me. It was Midge who'd said that Mr. Mullock feared me, but I hadn't believed him.

"I thought I'd be back in Botany Bay, or in my grave by now," said Mr. Mullock. "Well, that time is near now, isn't it? Come the twittering hour, we'll see the end. Look at them out there, Tom. Listen to the drums. There must be a thousand junglies, and a thousand more besides. You can't think you'll stop them with bedposts and chair legs, do you?"

"I mean to try," I said.

"And good for you," said he. "But this time tomorrow you'll be turning on a spit, roasting alive on a cannibal fire, and I'll be turning right beside you. Midgely and Gaskin too."

I didn't think Boggis had been listening, but he stopped, halfway between his windows. "That ain't true, Tom," he said. "It ain't the end for us, is it?"

I shook my head. "We can hold them off."

"Hah!" Mr. Mullock came back to my side. "Please, Tom. Give me the axe and we'll 'ave a feast tonight. If we're to be eaten tomorrow we might as well be stuffed."

"Do it, Tom," said Boggis. "I'm hungry as well."

I looked at my little pile of wooden spears and saw that it was hopeless. I tossed the axe at Mr. Mullock's feet, and—caring for nothing—lay down at Midgely's side. I hoped to sleep, but I didn't.

Mr. Mullock opened his can of cockles. He opened another of peas, another of mutton, and one of ham. He pierced them all with the axe, and sucked the tins like a great green fly.

Boggis ate with him, and Midgely too when he came awake, though at first he was leery. "It ain't ours," he said. "When the missionary comes home he'll be hopping mad."

Midge couldn't see the ruin and rot in the house. I told him, "I don't think he'll mind."

"Where do you suppose he is, Tom? Do you think he's at the feast?"

136

"Hah! No doubt," said Mr. Mullock, "'e *is* the feast."

Midgely laughed. "It ain't like that. He'll sort them out, those Indians. He'll tell them what's what."

We let Midgely think what he wanted; it did no harm. We gorged ourselves on sardines and clams, then Mr. Mullock—to my surprise—returned the axe to me. But I worked no more with the bedposts. I didn't wish to explain to Midge what I was doing.

The drums beat on, and the sunset came. We all stood at the west-facing window and watched it. The mountain seemed wreathed in fire, a volcano erupting, the mist that hovered over it now a scarlet smoke. It was, said Mr. Mullock, the finest sunset he'd ever seen. So gaudy was it that even Midge could see the colors. "It'll be a grand day tomorrow," he said. "Red sky at night, and all."

Slowly the colors faded, seeping away like fresh paint in a rain. To see the sprays of color turn to gray and black made me think how close we were to death, and how all our world and all we knew would fade away like that.

We stayed at the window, as though trying to cling to the waning light. But there was no stopping the blackness that settled round us, and soon it hid the savages beyond the walls, and then the walls themselves.

Boggis turned away. It was too sad to look out there, he said. Too scary and sad. So he didn't see the fires lit in the jungle, the great towers of flame—two and then four—that leapt up like creatures rising from the ground.

We saw them from above, through branches and leaves, but I was amazed to find how close the savages had been that day. We might have blundered right into their camp instead of the mission if we had landed—as Midgely had wanted—right on the shore below it.

Now, along with the drums, came the crackling and roar of the fires. And we saw the savages dance. Like insects drawn by the flames, they came whirling from the shadows; they writhed, they shouted, they bent and straightened, turned and jumped, all to a quickening beat of the drums. The long spears each of them held, they thrust into the air as though stabbing at the smoke and sparks.

It was a scene of utter wildness. It put fear in my heart to see it, in the hearts of all of us but Midgely.

"Are they dancing now?" he asked, and came to look for himself. Through a tunnel of his hands, he stared at blots of light.

"Come along, Midgely," said Mr. Mullock. There was no hint in his voice of the horror outside. He drew Midgely away with a hand on his shoulder. "We'll just sit 'ere and wait for the reverend to come 'ome."

So we all sat below the window, watching the light of the savages' fires play across the ceiling.

"Well, lads," said Mr. Mullock. "Someone might sing us a song if 'e likes."

I didn't think he meant to, but he made us remember Early. He coughed and said, "Maybe not. 'Ere, why don't you tuck into the grub. 'Ave a good talk. Pray if you've a mind to. Myself, I think I'd like a breath of fresh air." He got up.

"Where are you going?" I asked, suspicious already.

"Nowhere far," said he. "Tom, why don't you come and see the door's bolted behind me?"

We had to grope our way down the stairs. Mr. Mullock waited until we'd reached the bottom before he drew me close and talked in a hushed voice. "Look, Tom," he said. "What do you think's become of the reverend? Did they kill him or did he flee?"

"What difference does it make?" I asked.

"Well, I was wondering about 'is boat, Tom. If 'e's cooking in one of them fires, then shouldn't 'is boat still be 'ere?" Mr. Mullock's beard rasped against my cheek. "I thought I'd go and look."

"Alone?" said I.

His breath was hot, tainted by the food he'd eaten. "If you don't trust me to come back, Tom, then I'll stay 'ere and you can go. Up to you, my lad."

That put me on the spot. I didn't trust him all that far even then. What if he wanted to go alone so that he could find the steamboat and escape by himself? I didn't know what to say. I didn't *want* to go, but felt that I should. I would look like a coward if I didn't volunteer. So I did.

"I'm quicker than you, Mr. Mullock," I said. "My eyes are better. *I* should go."

Both his hands came to rest on my shoulders. "That's square of you, it is," he said. "Takes a brave lad to say that. But I can't allow it, Tom. You belong with young Midge. At dawn they'll come, and you should be at 'is side. You'll 'ave the axe. Make it quick for 'im, Tom."

"No. I could never do that," I said.

"You'll 'ave to," said he. "Lord knows that boy's suffered enough in 'is life. No point in 'im suffering at the end, not if you're there to 'elp 'im."

He touched the back of my neck. His finger—cold and rough—felt along my bones. "Right 'ere. That's the place," he said. "Give 'im a chop there, and 'e won't feel a thing."

We went together to the door. Together we went through it and out to the walled-in space. "We 'ave to 'urry," Mr. Mullock said. "We 'ave to race the moon."

Along the wall we scuttled. Round the corner to the gate. The drums were loud, the savages shrieking. Sparks soared high above our heads, and I fancied that the sky was brightening with the rising of the moon.

The bolts squealed in the gate. A bird—or a beast—a thing in the jungle, made nearly the same sound. Mr. Mullock worked the latches, drew the bolts, then cracked the gate and peered out. I pressed against him to see over his shoulder. One look was enough to tell us it couldn't be done. No one could reach the boat. The savages still stood at the edge of the clearing.

"Blast it," said Mr. Mullock. "What fool built this mission so far from the sea and left no way to get out? It was folly then, and folly now."

Off in the jungle, the shrieking rose to a fever pitch, the drumming to a frenzy. We locked the gate and drew back to the door. Just as we neared it, the drumming stopped.

"Good Lord," said Mr. Mullock.

And over the wall came the savages.

seventeen
TRAPPED IN MIDGELY'S MISSION

Mr. Mullock pushed me inside the mission. He came crashing in behind me, slammed the door, and latched it. I saw it shake on its hinges as something battered it from the other side.

"Are they attacking?" Midge cried out from upstairs.

Boggis's feet thudded on the stairs. "What's gone wrong?"

"Don't know. They never come at night," said Mr. Mullock. "They always wait for dawn. In every tale I've read or 'eard they come in the twittering hour."

At every window they appeared. From one came a puff of a sound, and a dart twanged into the wood beside me. From another came an arrow. The door banged and groaned until the whole house trembled.

"Get the axe," said Mr. Mullock. "Get the bedposts, boy."

How long did it last? Was it the hours that it seemed—or only minutes? Through the window slits we battled, thrusting with our sharpened sticks. Midgely stayed upstairs, flinging tins from the window, flinging down the flowerpot and anything else he found.

Mr. Mullock wielded the axe. He dashed from window to window, swinging it left and right, striking down anything that came through them. We shouted and yelled, and the savages screamed. Then, suddenly, all was quiet again.

Mr. Mullock was panting. "We carried the field," he said. "That time at least. Hah! They'll 'ave a fight to get us, lads."

In the middle of the night, the natives returned. By the light of the moon they surged over the wall, and up we got with our bedposts. As I hammered and thrust, I fell too close to a window, and an arm reached in and grabbed me. It jammed me into the slit, and Boggis tried to pull me back. A spear jabbed at me; an arrow went zinging past. Then Mr. Mullock's axe fell before my face, and I staggered away with a thing like a monstrous spider still clinging to my arm.

All that was in the house we hurled through the slits. The china and the cutlery, it all became our weapons. Then Midgely screamed from upstairs. "Tom, they're coming up!"

"Go and 'elp," said Mr. Mullock.

The building was shaking. The floor seemed to shift and buckle at my feet as I crossed it and hurried up the stairs. I saw Midgely standing by a window, and a savage scrambling over the sill. His face and arms were painted and tattooed, and he looked like a skeleton crawling through. I charged and drove him back. He fell howling to the ground.

Upstairs and down, the battle went on in clashes of wood and metal, in shouting voices and the smell of sweat. Then it was over again, and the air was still, as though a storm had raged and passed. But in the jungle, the drumming resumed.

I led Midgely downstairs. Like all of us, he knew that the end had come, that we couldn't hold out for very long. We had used everything at hand, and all of it was gone. Even the reverend's Bibles had been thrown through the windows. But Midgely wasn't frightened so much as dismayed. "Where's the reverend?" he kept saying. "Where's the reverend gone?"

Boggis had a cut on his arm. He clamped his hand over the wound, and the blood trickled through his fingers. "I hope the navy comes," he said. "Do you think they're looking for us, Mr. Mullock?"

"Hah!" said Mr. Mullock. "I'm sure they are, boy. But don't think they'll save us. I tell you I'm cursed. For seven years I've been doomed."

The moon floated in the window, bright and yellow, wider than the slit. Mr. Mullock looked solemn and sad. "Why are you cursed?" I asked.

"It doesn't matter, lad. Not now," he said. "Our time's measured in minutes, so live large, I say."

With that, he stood up. He climbed the stairs, and bustled about above us. We heard water being spilt from jug to basin, a few little grunts and oaths. Then down he came again, freshly shaven and shed of his strange green turtle skin. He wore, instead, the good clean clothes of the missionary. A rather battered beaver hat took the place of his helmet. In a morning coat and white cravat, in pinstriped trousers, he looked rather handsome. For once, he really did look like a lord.

He smiled at me. It was a true smile, one of pleasure and nothing more. It made me think that I'd misjudged him. If I had never met the Gypsy, had never ventured into the caves, I might have taken to him right away.

The moon drifted on. It left us in a gray light, and then in blackness when it set. We faced the darkest hours of the night, those before the dawn.

"Boys, I'll tell you that story," said Mr. Mullock. "About the fellow who went from rags to riches. I'll tell you how he was cursed."

"Is this fellow you?" I asked.

"Yes," he said, and began.

His story started in Plymouth. He was a Plymouth Mullock, he said, just as poor Early had guessed. "When I was twenty and one, I went off to London," he said. "I went to seek my fortune, and—lads—I tell you I found it. I—"

"Shhh!" said Midgely. "Listen; there ain't no drumming no more."

eighteen

THE LADY IN THE TREES

Out of the darkness, the savages came in such a wild rush that Mr. Mullock said they'd only been toying with us before. They came with their spears and their arrows, their breast-plates aglow. They came this time with torches.

At first it looked as though the whole jungle was burning. A wall of fire came toward us, bounding through the trees. It rippled across the clearing. It rose to the top of the logs, flowed over, and from end to end the stockade seemed to burst into flames.

The savages leapt to the ground. Some came straight to the house, pitching the torches against the wooden skirting. Others whirled them round in a rush and roar of fire, then sent them spinning upward. One clattered in through an up-stairs window, and the rest thudded on the roof. In moments, coils of smoke were drifting down the stairs. Then the thatching fell in a burning mass.

Every slit was wreathed in fire. We coughed and spluttered as the smoke thickened.

Midgely held his hands over his head. Boggis ran to a window. In the center of the room, Mr. Mullock was turning round and round, starting back from each new cloud of sparks and embers. The smoke glowed red and orange at his feet.

"I won't be burned," he said. "I'll be burning evermore, I think, and I can wait for Judgment Day. Come on, lads; let's see how many of the devils we can take with us."

He went to the door, shielding his eyes from the smoke. Boggis lumbered behind him, but I couldn't see Midgely. He'd moved from his place, and I couldn't see him anywhere. "Midge!" I shouted. "Midge, where are you?"

If he answered, I didn't hear him. But at last I saw him sitting cross-legged on the floor. He was sucking his thumb, and he rocked back and forth. He looked so tiny sitting all by himself in the smoke. "Oh, Midge," I cried, and started toward him.

He seemed to rise from the floor. His legs didn't move, and his arms didn't move, but he lifted straight up nonetheless. I saw the floor itself bubble up, a bulge forming in the planks. Nails popped out; wood splintered, and a huge round head came bursting through the floor.

Midge screamed. "Help me, Tom!" he shouted.

Entire planks split and cracked. In the bang of breaking wood, the jarring squeal of torn-out nails, they exploded from their joists, springing out along their lengths. And up through the hole that head kept rising, a monstrous snake battered into the mission.

Each of its scales seemed as big as my hand, and they rippled and coursed as the head swung around. The eyes were huge and yellow, the tongue a long flicker like the fire of the dragons.

Midgely tried to scuttle away. But the snake's head writhed in a half circle, rearing above him. The tongue shot out, the great jaws opened, and that beast swallowed Midgely whole. I saw his legs kicking, then one of his shoes go flying, until there was nothing left of him at all.

The snake eased back, sinking into the hole. The planks began to settle in their places, then suddenly shot in all directions as the creature lunged again. Its head rose three feet, five feet, six feet from the floor. It nearly touched the ceiling, then slowly swung and lowered. A hump of the body came after it, like a sea serpent surfacing, and soon all its length stretched in curls from wall to wall. The tail swept like a whip, smashing the staircase in a cloud of embers. The head came slithering toward me.

For a moment I was looking straight in the serpent's eyes. I saw its neck ripple as the head drew back only to surge forward and slam against my chest. I flew off my feet, thudding to the floor. The jaws opened again, and they closed around my knees.

I tried to pull away, but couldn't. I felt its muscles pulsing, sucking me inside.

Boggis and Mr. Mullock seemed turned to stone. Flames

were licking round the edges of the door, and smoke was spouting underneath. The latch and bolt glowed red from the heat.

"Help!" I shouted. The snake's lips had reached to my thighs.

Its body arched and rippled. The tail struck the ceiling, slammed on the floor, then coiled around Boggis and Mr. Mullock too. It enveloped them both, then doubled and doubled again as it rolled them up in its coils.

Mr. Mullock hammered with his axe, but the snake only wrapped another coil around him.

"Tom!" he cried. "Catch, my boy!"

He threw the axe to me. It bounced from the floor and landed just beyond my reach. Though I stretched every bone in my arm and my fingers, I couldn't quite touch it.

I tried to kick the snake. I shook and struggled, but it only swallowed me more quickly, its muscles kneading at my feet and legs. Then with a flick of its head I was swept sideways and pushed along the floor, and I grabbed the axe.

My arms couldn't reach the creature's head, so I had to wait as the thing consumed more of me. Then as I slid into its mouth, up to my waist, up to my ribs, I drove the axe down with both hands onto the creature's head. I struck it hard, and again. I pierced the mound of its nose, wrenched out the blade, and struck again.

Such a tremor shot through the snake that I thought it would crush me. The lips tightened like a vice, and I could scarcely draw a breath. But I kept jabbing at it, aiming for the eyes, striking again and again and again. And as it swung me in a huge arc, across the width of the room, I pierced its nose. I pierced an eye. Dark blood squirted out. Like the spout of a whale it spewed from the thing. Then, with a last shake and a tremble, the enormous snake fell flat.

With my legs I pried the jaws apart. I squirmed backward from its mouth.

I wasted no time. As Mr. Mullock and Boggis freed themselves from the creature's coils, I slashed the belly open. I ripped the axe through scales and skin, and that terrible thing fell open. Out tumbled Midgely. His hands were folded on his face, his elbows pressed at his side. I couldn't hear him breathing; there seemed no life in him at all.

I picked up his limp body. It was so small and light—so cold. I held him in my arms, and thought I would just sit and hold him until the building burned down upon us. But Mr. Mullock hauled him from me. He held him up, his hands under Midgely's armpits, and shook him furiously. He pulled him close for a moment, then laid him on the floor, raised a hand and slapped him. Three times he hit the boy, hard and fast. "Come on!" he said. "Breathe."

Again, he slapped Midgely. His fingers left bright red smears on the cheek. Then Midgely trembled. He coughed; he drew in a whistling breath. "Oh, Midge!" I cried.

I put my arms around him. I struggled to lift him up. "We have to hurry," I said.

"Hurry? Hah!" said Mr. Mullock. "Hurry to where?"

"If that snake came in," I said, "we can surely get out."

Boggis had taken up the axe and was slashing at the snake. He tore long slices through its belly, and things were

149

falling out: a big, round rock; a coconut; a wooden box and a grotesquely rotted pig; an old umbrella with mere shreds of cloth clinging to its wires; a little pair of spectacles.

What possessed me I couldn't imagine, but I had to have those things. I picked them up as if they were fallen treasures, or bits of myself. I took the wooden box and the umbrella. I took the spectacles too. I would have taken the rock and the coconut, but I heard the axe ripping through the snake's flesh, and knew that the next thing to spill out would be the corpse of the missionary.

I came somewhat to my senses then, but not enough to cast off my frivolous finds. I pulled Boggis away. "Let's go," I said.

With a crash and searing heat, half the upper floor collapsed. The rest creaked and shifted as we flung ourselves down through the shattered hole in the floor. No sooner had we fallen into the space below the house than the entire structure collapsed on top of itself.

We fell from thick smoke into clear air. A breeze—a wind—why, half a gale moaned through the space. "The fire's sucking air," said Mr. Mullock. "There's a passage leading into here."

It was easy to find; we crawled into the wind, and the ground sloped down. Our shadows stretched in front of us, vanishing as the firelight faded. In pitch blackness we found ourselves in a vast cellar that smelled of earth, then in a tunnel that led us straight to the sea. We came out through a band of bushes and emerged at the edge of the jungle.

Ahead was a mangrove swamp, the strange trees marching off into the water. Behind, we could see the mission burning, the savages watching the flames. I judged that it would be hours before the ashes would give away the secret of our escape. I felt free and happy. But my joy was short-lived.

"There's no boat," said Mr. Mullock.

"There must be." I looked down at the water as though he might have overlooked a steamboat sitting there. But the glare of flames reached far through the trees, and I had to admit that he was right. If a boat had been floating anywhere near, we would have seen it in the firelight. "What do we do?" I asked.

"What do you think?" Mr. Mullock held his hands apart, as though to show me the living arches and tangles of the mangroves. "We can't go by sea, and we can't go back. We'll have to make our stand right here."

"Maybe the junglies won't come looking," said Boggis.

"Hah!"

Midgely waded into the water, in among the mangroves. He splashed and rubbed himself, cleaning off the slimy wetness from the innards of the snake. "I don't understand none of this," he said. "The Indians here ain't vicious."

"Well, thank God we found the gentle ones then," said Mr. Mullock. His fine new clothes were already filthy.

"And where's the missionary?" asked Midge. "Why ain't he here to take us away? You don't think his whole book and all was nonsense do you, Tom? You don't think it was all a pack of lies, do you? Maybe he was never here at all."

"He was," I said. "But, Midge, he's gone. He's . . ." I put the umbrella in his hands. He felt along the wires and along the handle, and his face seemed understanding.

"I found his spectacles too," I said. "And this wooden box."

It had a small latch of dulled brass. I flicked that aside, raised the lid, and took out a thing like old, squashed parchment. It was nearly transparent. I didn't know what it was, and neither did Mr. Mullock. But Midgely grinned as soon as he touched it.

"There *is* a boat here," he said. "There must be a boat."

"He's gone daft," said Mr. Mullock.

"Look!" said Midgely. He held up that thing from the box. "It's a caul, ain't it? The reverend, he went back for his caul when the snake got him."

I had no idea what he meant. His hands were shaking, and he was hopping up and down in the shallows. "This come off a baby when it was born," he said. "It covered the face of a baby. Don't you see?"

"No," I said.

"A baby's caul! A man's safe from drowning if he's got a caul," said Midge. "He wouldn't never go to sea without it, would he? So the boat's still here."

With that, he turned and waded through the mangroves. In a few steps he was up to his waist, feeling ahead of himself, and all around, with the shredded old umbrella. He poked it up and poked it down, and swept it side to side. He tapped it on the great roots of the trees. "Come on," he said, and beckoned us to follow.

Nothing could be more strange and eerie than a stand of mangroves, except a stand of mangroves lit by fire. The roots soared above us, taking on fantastic shapes. They looked like the arches and domes of a Gothic church, and like the limbs of strange creatures. They seemed to move, to walk, always changing in the shifting light. And the trees creaked and swayed, while every creature in them chattered and clicked and whined.

Midgely led us left and right, tapping all the way. We tried to stay close to him but struggled to keep up. The trees were so densely spaced, their branches so tangled, that we were soon as blind as he.

Something hissed above us. Midgely squealed. "No!" he shouted, and threw himself flat in the water.

I looked up. There was a yellow glow among the branches, a pale shape in the middle, and a white face peering out. Then a person stood up—a person or a phantom; for a moment I wasn't sure—a figure of white emerging from the tangle. I gasped. Arms reached out; clothing fluttered. It seemed impossible, but there was a lady up there, a blond-headed lady in a white bonnet and shawls.

Mr. Mullock saw her—Boggis too—and we all stared at this lady in white. "Simon," she hissed. "Simon, are you there?"

Mr. Mullock pulled off his new hat. He bowed as he greeted the lady. "Mr. Mullock, at your service."

An odder scene I could never have imagined. As the old mission burned to the ground, the savages gathered around it, the four of us stood in a half-drowned forest, talking to a lady who seemed to float like an angel in the trees. But she didn't seem put out. "Please come up," she said. "The ladder's to your left."

"Where is she?" Midgely asked. "Is she up in a tree house, Tom?"

It seemed that way at first. The ladder was made of sticks nailed to a tree trunk, climbing into a framework of timbers. Halfway up, I thought I saw a shining house of varnished wood tucked among the branches and the leaves. It was not until I reached the top that I saw it was a steamboat.

It was a grand little boat, polished and bright, its machinery gleaming. Every inch was jammed with lengths of firewood, all precisely sawn and neatly stacked. They lay along the sides, under the seats, and up in the bow, and leaned against the curved dome that covered the paddle wheels. Only a small space was left around the engine, and another at the curved seat in the stern, where a candle was burning in a short silver stick. A Bible lay open beside it. The lady was standing there, reaching over the side to help me.

The boat sat firm and steady on the timbers. They served both as a cradle and a launching ramp, while a heavy tackle fixed to the tree held the boat in place. As soon as he touched it, Midge knew it was a boat. "You see?" he cried. "I told you it was here."

The lady looked at him. She was younger and prettier than I'd ever known my mother to be, but the expression was one my mother had worn many times in the years before her madness. It was a look at once of loving and worry and care, and I felt instantly heartsick.

She put her hand on Midgely, but spoke to Mr. Mullock. Her voice was very lovely. "Tell me," she said. "What of Mr. Collins?"

"Your husband, missus?" he asked.

"The Reverend Collins," said she. "Oh, please tell me; have you seen him?"

Mr. Mullock stood bare-headed before her, the reverend's own hat turning in his hands. "Not hexactly, missus," he said. "But I believe he's . . . Well, he's gone to his maker, missus."

She sighed. Delicately, she sank to the seat. Her hand was still on Midgely's shoulder, and she pulled him with her, so that they sat side by side. "I feared as much," she said. "I begged him not to go back. But he wouldn't leave without his silly caul."

Midge looked up with a triumphant smile. "Is it the same Simon Collins what wrote a book, mum?" he asked.

She uttered a funny little laugh that was half a sob. "Oh, his book," she said. "How I came to loathe it. Do you know it was the book that brought him to the islands?"

Midgely looked puzzled. "But he wrote it. How . . ."

She stroked Midgely's arm. "We'll talk of it later, child. Tell me, can one of you operate a steamboat?"

Mr. Mullock bowed again. "You're haddressing a dab hand with the steamboats, missus. Hah! It's a fortunate day indeed."

How quickly he could change. Not an hour before, he'd been preparing for his end. Now he was all charm. With a wink and a smile, he took her candle and held it to the engine, peering at all the polished pipes and other bits, giving each one a poke and a studious "hmmm."

"The boiler's full," he pronounced. "The firebox too. I can 'ave her steam up in a moment. Here, you muggins, give me a 'and."

It was me he meant. He got me kneeling beside him, at the door of the firebox. "You'll tend to it," he said. "Keep it stuffed, boy; we'll need every inch of steam."

155

He touched the candle to the wood. The sticks were tinder dry, and the flames spread quickly along them. I threw in some more wood and closed the door. A small window let me watch the fire.

"We've only an hour till dawn," said Mr. Mullock. "We'll 'ave to 'urry."

He and Boggis launched the boat, easing it down the rails. They pushed and pulled it through the mangroves, then came aboard when we were clear of the trees and the ocean was empty before us. Mr. Mullock held his candle to a little gauge where a needle quivered on a dial. He tapped a small lever, then pushed on a larger one. With a thump and a hiss, the engine went to its work.

A piston moved. A crank swung round. Below the curved hood, paddle wheels were turning, and with a splash of water the boat moved forward. It all seemed too loud to me—a clicking, clacking din that was bound to alert the natives. But the boat chugged along, and what wind there was blew from behind us, gusting our smoke ahead.

There was a tiller in the stern, and Mr. Mullock sat by it. He steered us from the island, and I stuffed the firebox full, then raised my head and looked back.

Where the mission had been was a great glow of embers, a fountain of sparks that shot glittering rockets into the air. Among the trees, the smaller fires of the savages winked and blinked like many red eyes. It was all I could see. Not even the loom of the land was visible, and the sky was solid black.

nineteen
NEWS OF REDMAN TIN

In the daylight our boat was a beautiful thing. Inside and out it was varnished and polished, and it chugged along at a good clip. The missionary's island, only a slit of green at dawn, had vanished soon after. But a pall of smoke stretched behind us, for the wind had fallen calm.

The engine puffed and rattled. The paddle wheels thumped, and the water foamed along the hull. I watched the sea split at the bow, the bubbles rushing by, and guessed that a cantering horse wouldn't have gone any faster.

I was the only one with a chore. The fire demanded endless work, and I carried wood—and bent and straightened—until my every muscle ached. Each time I opened the firebox, the heat was a sweltering blow to my face. Oh, how I loathed Mr. Mullock then, sprawled as he was on the big seat in the stern. He was so lazy that he lay back and steered with his foot, and now and then dipped a hand into the sea to sprinkle cooling dribbles on his neck and hair.

Boggis slept, snoring as loudly as the engine. Midgely leaned against the lady, who sat bolt upright on the stern seat, as far as she could be from Mr. Mullock and still be sitting there. Her arm was draped round Midgely.

"The poor little dear," she said. "He's not made for the sun and the heat."

She touched his cheeks. They were red and blistered, but I imagined mine were much the same, and maybe worse. As I put more wood in the box, I imagined my eyebrows were being singed away.

"It's shocking," she said. "We have to do something for him."

She set about it right then, turning the missionary's umbrella into a parasol for Midgely. She hoisted her skirts and tore away a bit of her petticoat—there seemed miles of it under there—and didn't Mr. Mullock's eyes grow wide? The biggest effort he made that morning was to drop his jaw and gape.

The lady plucked the old bits of cloth from the umbrella wires. She let them flutter from her fingertips and drift away.

"Was that the reverend's?" asked Mr. Mullock, who already knew that it was. "Did you say 'e was your husband, missus?"

"Good gracious, no," she said. "I'm Lucy Beans. Lucy Elizabeth Beans."

"A pleasure," said Mr. Mullock, with a tip of his head.

She ignored him. "I was the nanny. Until Mrs. Collins up and left, and took the children with her. Why, that was not a week ago. Fancy that, Mr. Mullock."

I'd thought Midgely was asleep, but he wasn't. He tipped up his head. "Why didn't you go with them, mum?"

"And leave the reverend behind?" She patted him fondly. "The poor doddering fellow. If you'd met him, you wouldn't be asking that."

I wished I could change places with Midgely. She was the prettiest lady I'd ever seen.

"I never cared for Mrs. Collins," she said. "No surprise to me that she took the first chance to leave. When the ship came, she was on it in a streak."

"What ship was that?" I asked.

"Oh, a big brown ship," said she. "The captain was very kindly. I wish I knew his name."

"Was it Tin?" I asked. "Redman Tin?"

Boggis frowned. "That's *your* name, Tom," he said.

"Huh!" barked Mr. Mullock. "So that's why you're so keen to meet this ship."

"Well, no wonder," said Lucy Beans. She opened the umbrella. "But I'm sorry, Tom, I never heard the man's name. I only called him Captain, and I saw him only briefly. He had an errand in the islands, and didn't tarry long."

"What errand, miss?" I asked.

"He was most mysterious about it." She ran her fingers through the wires. "He had a talk with the reverend. Then he was off—quick as that. Oh, in a great hurry he was. Afraid he was too late already."

It had to have been my father; I was certain of it. He must have called at the mission, searching either for me or for the island where we'd agreed to find each other.

"Where did he go?" I asked.

Mr. Mullock grunted. "Your fire wants tending, you muggins."

"Why, the boy's worn ragged," said Lucy. "Why don't *you* tend the fire, Mr. Mullock?"

"I would," said he. "Hah! But I'm steering."

With a sigh, she put down the umbrella. "I shall tend it myself."

"I wouldn't 'ear of it," said Mr. Mullock. There was a toothed strip of metal set into the back of the boat, and he fitted the tiller to that. Then he rolled himself from the seat, stood up, stretched, and promptly kicked Gaskin Boggis awake. He put *him* to work instead.

I was happy to pass on the chores, happier still when Lucy Beans patted the seat and said, "Sit up beside me, dear."

Content as a cat, I settled there. The smoke puffed up from the engine and wafted over our heads. The sea went burbling past. "I like this boat," I said. "It's beautiful."

"The reverend's pride and joy." She picked up the umbrella and laid her petticoat across it. "He brought it out from England so that he might putter round the islands. The girls loved it too. Katy, the youngest, called it *Chickadee*."

It was a splendid name. The engine made just that sound. As I eased back, exhausted, I heard the name repeated over and over in the rattle of cranks, the sigh and puff of steam. *Chickadee. Chuckatee. Chuckatee-chickadee.* It lulled me into sleep.

When I woke, all had changed. Midgely was steering, and Mr. Mullock—for once—was sitting like a proper person, his arm stretched behind Midgely. "Now, you're wandering again," he said. "But for a blind boy you're doing rather well."

Midgely was smiling. His face was all in shadow, for above it Lucy Beans was holding the umbrella, now turned to a delicate parasol.

"Where are you heading?" I asked.

"I don't even know, Tom," he said. "But ain't it grand?"

The compass was arranged so that only Mr. Mullock could see it. When I leaned over, he crossed his legs, blocking my view of the dial.

"Lucy, how long did you live on the island?" he asked.

"A year and a half," said she. "It was an idyll, Mr. Mullock. There was a village nearby, just a handful of houses. Katy and Mae, they played with the Indian children."

"With the cannibals?" asked Mr. Mullock.

She laughed. "Hardly. They were the sweetest people. Then those *savages* came. Just a few days ago, I think. They came in a huge canoe with a roof and—gracious!—I don't know how many rowers. They . . ." She put her hand to her eyes. "I can't bear to think of the horror."

"I *knew* the Indians here was friendly," crowed Midgely. "That was in his book, mum."

"By chance, then," she said. "That silly book. I called it his fairy tale."

Poor Midgely. His smile faded; his face collapsed. "It isn't true, mum?" he said.

"How could it be? He wrote it in England." She tilted the

161

parasol. "He wrote down the tales of the vagabonds. He plied them with spirits, and they obliged with the wildest stories. But the poor dear took them to heart, and the day he finished that book he told us we were going to see the islands."

Midgely was crestfallen, but the news was worse for me. It meant I was seeking my father, and he seeking me, in a strange, invented land. I felt suddenly close to tears. "Is there no island that looks like an elephant?" I asked. "There must be one. I'm supposed to find my father there."

She smiled so kindly. "If it must be so, it's so," she said.

"Hah!" barked Mr. Mullock.

"Hush, you!" she said. "The reverend didn't invent things wholly. If he wrote of an elephant island, it was because the vagabonds told him of one. It might not be where he said it is, but it's sure to be somewhere."

Precious good that did for me. I looked all around the horizon, but couldn't see a speck of land. Boggis, in his mindless way, was feeding wood to the fire, and the boat was carrying us on. I had no idea where we were, or whither we were going.

I looked at Midgely steering blindly, at Mr. Mullock glancing at his compass. Then, in the varnished wood, I saw the dial reflected.

"North!" I said. "You're going north again."

He looked surprised, but only for a moment. "Yes," he said. "I'm taking Miss Beans to Shanghai."

She repeated the name. "Shanghai? Could there be a place more wild and wicked?"

"I fancy not," said Mr. Mullock, with a grin.

"No, not since Sodom and Gomorrah," said she. "Why, I

wouldn't go there if it were the last place on earth. What are you thinking, Mr. Mullock?"

"I . . . ," he said, faltering. "I thought . . . I wanted . . . Well, you see . . ."

"Where's this elephant island?" she asked.

"More to the east," I said.

"Then steer to the east," she commanded.

Mr. Mullock didn't argue. He hauled on the tiller, and the bow swung around. The smoke streamed sideways for a moment, then fell in line again behind us. For nearly an hour I could look back and see the sudden bend in its path. Slowly that dissolved, and there was nothing to show that we had ever being going anywhere but east. The horizon ahead was empty.

twenty

OUR ENCOUNTER WITH THE SAVAGES

We burned through our wood at a staggering rate. Mr. Mullock said we could keep up our speed, or spare the wood, but not do both. "If we run 'er slowly we might go for days," he said. "But isn't speed of the hessence 'ere?"

"Indeed," said Lucy Beans.

In the afternoon, a group of islands appeared ahead. They slid toward us on the moving sea, and drew alongside in the evening. The lady made a game of trying to find their hidden shapes, making Midgely giggle with her guesses. "Is that a goose in a bowler hat?" she said. "And look. Isn't that Mr. Mullock? See his big nose?" She saw many things, but not an elephant, and her game lapsed into a dreary sadness.

We chuffed along until dark, then didn't really land at all. We found a place where the shore was steep and wooded, then tethered the boat to a branch. Mr. Mullock opened the firebox and took out the burning wood. There was a pair of tongs for that purpose, and with those he plunged each stick into the sea. It steamed and hissed, and the water bubbled. Then he lifted the blackened bit—still wet and smoking—and set it in a bucket. The wood had a curious smell, quite tart and strong, that reminded me of gunpowder.

We slept in the boat, in a horde of insects that swarmed below the trees. Mr. Mullock said there might be pythons, and that we should be on our guard. "They like to drop down and stun you," he said.

"Mercy me," said Lucy. "But you'll stand watch through the night, won't you, Mr. . . . What's your Christian name, Mr. Mullock?"

"Ernie," he said simply.

In his dark clothes, with his white shirt underneath, a pale strip was all I could see of him. He was standing when I fell asleep, but not when I woke in the morning, and it was soon plain to all that he hadn't kept a very long watch. He was more rested than anyone, and eager to be off.

We stoked the fire and steamed along the shore, to a beach where tall palms were growing. Mr. Mullock reversed the engine to keep us off the shore. "You and you," he said to Boggis and me. "Hop out and get some wood."

It was easier said than done. We rummaged through the undergrowth, but found only soft and rotted wood. In the end, Mr. Mullock had to come and help us—for Lucy Beans made him do it. He waded ashore with a long, two-handled saw. The boat sat still in the water, under a thin plume of smoke, the hull reflecting all the colors of the sea.

Mr. Mullock hefted the saw. "Might as well kill two birds with a stone, as my mother would say."

We felled one of the palms. Boggis and I did the sawing, and we did the bucking too, while Mr. Mullock went chasing the coconuts that rolled on the sand. But to give him his due, he didn't shirk. He carried the coconuts out to the boat, then carried the wood as we cut it. Back and forth he trudged, looking all the time along the beach and up to the trees. "Hurry, lads," he said. "There'll be junglies about."

When the tree was cut and stowed, and there'd been no sign of savages, we felled another. It crashed to the sand, bounced and crashed back. Boggis and I began sawing.

We'd gone halfway up the trunk when the savages arrived. They were suddenly on the beach, a silent group armed with spears, twenty and two in their cloths and feathers. But one wore a brown shirt, and another brown trousers, and from the neck of a third—as though a strange trophy—hung an old leather shoe on a string.

I knew convict clothes when I saw them. These seemed too big for Weedle or Carrots or Penny, but I couldn't be certain. I had no doubt, though, what fate had befallen the poor convict who'd once been inside them. He was now inside their new owner.

"Keep away, you damned junglies!" shouted Mr. Mullock. "Come no closer now, you hear?" Like a peahen, he seemed to believe that loudness made him frightening. "Face them, lads. Ease back toward me."

We did as he said. Boggis held the saw, and together we stepped down the sand. As we closed together, the savages spread apart. They formed a line, a curve that stretched past us on either side. We hurried backward, and barely gained the water before the curve could become a circle that enclosed us. The savages milled closer. One pointed at Mr. Mullock and jabbered away in his strange tongue.

"No understandee!" shouted Mr. Mullock, shaking his head furiously.

The savage tugged his breastplate and, pointing again at Mr. Mullock, babbled even louder.

"No understandee!" said Mr. Mullock again. "Me speakee English, you thick-wit!"

From the boat, Lucy Beans called out. "If you think you're speaking his tongue, you're mistaken, Mr. Mullock. He's saying he likes your clothing. He admires your coat and vest, and says he'll trade his for yours."

"He does, does he? Hah!" Mr. Mullock waved his hands. "Lookee; no tradee!" he shouted at the savage. "Understandee? No tradee!"

"Please," I said. "Give him your coat."

"Not on your life," said Mr. Mullock. "Give him that, it will be my heart and liver next. Back, lads. A step back."

We splashed into the water. The savages came closer. The talking one shook his spear, then hammered the shaft against his breastplate. All the little bones and things he wore rattled at his chest.

"We'll dash for it, lads. On my word," said Mr. Mullock. I could hear his breaths. "Now!"

He was first to run. Before I'd turned to follow, the savages were upon us. They grabbed; they pulled and pushed. Mr. Mullock was hauled down, and with six around him he floundered in the water. Boggis and I tried to help.

"Stop that!" cried Lucy Beans. She put a hand up to the engine, and with a gout of steam there came a piercing shriek of a sound. It loosed a mad chorus from the island, and shocked the savages into silence. Then, in a voice just as piercing, Lucy cried out in the same tongue as theirs. On and on she went, and like a lot of sheepish boys they hung their heads. They eased away. I wouldn't have been surprised if they'd picked up our wood and loaded it into the steamboat. But it didn't go as far as that. One answered with a few clipped words, then all trotted together into the forest.

Mr. Mullock rose from the sea, looking half drowned and white as death. His splendid new hat was floating upside down, rocking like a small coracle. He picked it up and put it on. "Leave the wood," he said. "We're clearing off."

Lucy helped us into the boat. She fussed with Mr. Mullock, who was certainly the wettest of us all, but she saved her warmest smile for me. "That Indian." She nodded toward the land. "He said your elephant island is three days to the east."

"He did? He told you that?" I looked into her eyes, surprised by the color—a green as bright as grass. "That's wonderful, miss."

"Hah!" barked Mr. Mullock. "Now they know where we're going. Damned junglies. They'll be waiting."

"Oh, Ernie, no." She turned back to him. His hat had gotten a bit crushed, and she took it from his head to smooth the puckers in the crown. "They only fancied your clothes."

"And my skin, and my 'ead."

"They didn't," she said with a laugh. "If they'd fancied that handsome head, you wouldn't be standing here with it now, I'll tell you that. What they want, they take." She returned his hat, tipping it at a rakish slant. "But not all the Indians are savages, Ernie. They're quite nice people, most of them. It's only the headhunters and cannibals you have to fear. And the pirates, of course. They're much worse."

Midgely had been listening. "There weren't no pirates in the reverend's book, mum," he said.

"No vagabonds ever spoke of them, that's why," said Lucy Beans. "No one who has met the pirates has ever lived to speak again."

It was a frightening thought, made more frightening by the way she said it—with her voice low and her green eyes darting. Seeing how she'd scared us, she forced a laugh. "But don't worry, boys. In a year and a half I've yet to see a pirate. I'm sorry I spoke."

So was I. With a glance at the sea, a glance at the land, I bent down and shoved wood in the firebox. I got the engine pouring smoke, its little valves chattering, and when Mr. Mullock threw the lever, we bounded off with the paddle wheels churning.

We steamed through the islands at top speed. The boat left a long streak of foam on the water, another streak of smoke in the air, and the two merged behind us. The sound of the engine was a steady roar, now a *chuckateechick-adeechuckateechickadee*. It meant that we went through our stacks of wood the way a fat lady goes through a box of chocolates, but I didn't mind. I stuffed one stick after another into the firebox, and the engine gobbled them up, and the door was rarely closed.

At night we slowed down, but didn't stop. Two of us were

always awake, one steering and watching, the other caring for the boat. It was like a living thing that had to be fed and watered.

But it had to be rested too, and that became clear in the morning. There was steam jetting out where it hadn't before. Along with the hiss and huff and thump was a rattling ping that grew louder. Boggis, who'd been sitting quite close to the engine, moved as far as he could into the bow. I began to feed the thing as I might a crocodile—chucking the wood from a distance—for it suddenly seemed dangerous to be near it.

We ran the boat slowly as we searched for a place to land. When we saw bright beaches of sand, we turned away. We sought, instead, the darker places, and found the perfect island when we came to one that had no beach at all. Twice we circled it. Twice we headed toward the low cliff that formed its entire shore, and waited to see what emerged from the jungle.

The only thing to show its face was a small monkey. With tiny hands it spread the branches. With enormous eyes it peered at us, looking like a lost and lonely child.

Again we steamed around the island. That little monkey came with us, swinging now by his hands and now by his tail, keeping up a constant chatter. When we found a place of overhanging branches, and put the boat against the cliff, the monkey leapt straight down. It made right for Mr. Mullock, bounded up the back of his trousers, and clung tightly to his neck.

To say he was startled wouldn't be the half of it. He cried out as though a savage had attacked him, and the sight of him capering around with that tiny, wide-eyed creature made us laugh. Midgely didn't understand—how could he?—until the lovely Lucy described it all in a fashion so humorous that even Mr. Mullock had to smile.

"You've made a friend," she said. "You must have a good heart, Ernie, for animals to take to you like this."

I remembered his bat. He'd treated it with kindness, killed it with cruelty, then missed it very much. He was a hard one to fathom, that Mr. Mullock. But as he stood smiling in his gentleman's clothes, with the monkey clinging to his neck, I saw why Lucy seemed to like him.

We all climbed up to the island to look for wood and water. "It shall be like a picnic," said Lucy, and it was. We ate fruit straight from the tree, and Mr. Mullock had no choice but to share his. The monkey snatched what he wanted with the funniest and cheekiest of cries.

It was soon apparent that the island was empty of people, apart from us. I thought that we might well have been the only ones who had ever stood upon it, for none of its creatures showed the slightest sign of fear. The birds came down and ate the half-finished fruit we tossed aside. A wild pig snuffled through the glade where we rested. A frog sat nearly at Lucy's side, its throat pulsing, as though it were just another—a small green other—member of our party.

We strolled right around the island, then up to its low summit. Unlike previous islands, it was peaceful and beautiful, and even Midgely could tell—by the scents and the sounds—that we'd come to a place that was special.

"This is what the reverend was looking for," said Lucy. She gathered her skirts and sat down. "I wish he'd found this place; he would have been so happy. It's like the Garden of Eden, isn't it, Ernie?"

"It is," said Mr. Mullock, settling himself beside her.

Midgely had brought his parasol. When he sat it covered him completely, like a giant toadstool. I managed to find some shade below it too. Only Boggis was standing, staring off to the east.

"Ain't that a sail out there?" he asked.

twenty-one
MR. MULLOCK'S MYSTERIOUS PAST

Where Boggis pointed, I saw the sail. My first thought was of pirates, but Lucy Beans dismissed it. She said the pirate ships came from Borneo, that they wore black sails—one black sail to each mast. This was an English ship, or so Mr. Mullock named it right away. We could see only the topsails and royals, square and bright in the distance. It wasn't the worn, sun-bleached cloth of my father's ship, but the crisp new canvas of a man-of-war.

"The navy," said Mr. Mullock. "It's my curse to find a place like this and 'ave the navy 'unt me down."

Lucy looked up at him. "Why would the navy hunt you now? And why would you be cursed?"

Mr. Mullock settled back, staring up at the sky. I thought he wouldn't speak, but he closed his eyes and began the same story he'd begun at the mission. "When I was one and twenty, I went away to London," he said.

It must have taken him an hour to tell the whole tale. The monkey sat for a while on his chest, then lay on its side with its head in the curve of his neck. He reached out to touch it, and the monkey closed its tiny fist around the tip of his little finger. Lucy Beans moved closer to him, so that she too might pet and stroke the creature's khaki-colored head. She let Mr. Mullock talk, interrupting only now and then.

The first time was when he said, "I made an honest living dealing in the jewels of the ladies I hencountered."

"What does that mean?" she said, lifting her head from the grass.

"You might say I hintroduced the pawnman to their jewels, Lucy."

"Means he was a bug hunter, mum," said Midgely below his parasol.

"I weren't nothing of the sort," said Mr. Mullock. "Oh, you might say I 'oisted their jewels, and sometimes their silver and whatnot. I pawned them quick enough; it's true. But every farthing went back to the ladies. I kept not a penny for myself. I wined and dined them and took them off on the tour."

"Such kindness," she said.

"So it was," said he. "Everything they'd always wished for, I gave them. Italy; they saw it. France; they carriaged across it. My mother always said that money makes money, and so it did for me. I yachted on the Solent; I dined in clubs and breakfasted in castles, and didn't I grow as rich as a lord? Why, I *became* a lord. Hah! I did. I bought a lordship, Lucy. Lord Mullock of Duck End Green."

"Was there a Lady Mullock?" asked Lucy.

"Never. Oh, I 'ad my choice. Hah! Any lady I wished. But I've never met one who happealed to me in that fashion."

"Never?" she asked in a little voice.

He looked in her green eyes. "Never in London, I mean."

In the distance, as Mr. Mullock told his tale, the warship passed from island to island. The topsails sank below the horizon, then so did the topgallants, until only the small squares of the royals could be seen.

"I went from rags to riches," he said. "I'd started out as a stonemason. Did I tell you that? I built walls all over Devon in my youth. But in London I became something of an hexpert in jewels, I may say, and soon enough people came to me. Then I began to 'ear whisperings of the most fabulous stone of them all. It 'ad disappeared some time before, and in 'alf a century not a soul 'ad seen it."

A prickling came to the back of my neck. I sat up and listened, enthralled, certain I knew how the tale would end.

"There was talk that a young man 'ad found it," said Mr. Mullock. "Then 'e sent 'is card around, and I went off to see 'im. It was along the Strand somewhere, a fine part of the city. My knock was answered by a shriveled, decrepit man, a shuffling 'orror. I asked by name for the young fellow who 'ad sent for me. This old man said—and I shall never forget it—'I am 'e.' " Mr. Mullock swallowed and shivered. "Well, 'e was not yet thirty, but 'e 'ad more than one foot in the grave, I can tell you. Leprosy, it might have been."

"Gracious," said Lucy.

"The fellow took me in. Such filth. All 'is furniture was gone; not a stick was left. 'E lived like an animal in this shell of a fine 'ouse. I tell you, 'is own waste lay in a fly-ridden pile in the corner. I wanted none of it, and I turned to leave. Then I saw the stone. It sat on a shelf. It sat in the shadows, but—oh!—'ow it sparkled. I asked 'im 'is price. The figure 'e named was better than a bargain. It would 'ave been a swindle to 'ave bought it for that. Then he saw my 'esitation, and he 'alved the price. 'Take it, Lord Mullock,' said 'e. 'I beg you to take it.' "

"Whyever why?" asked Lucy.

"Oh, 'e loathed it," said Mr. Mullock. " 'It brings ruination, Lord Mullock. It brings misery,' said 'e. 'Misery and suffering and pain and death.' "

"I wouldn't have touched it," she said.

"Hah! You would if you'd seen it. It glowed with light. It pulsed on the shelf like a dark little 'eart. As soon as I saw that stone, I knew it 'ad to be mine."

He lay there, under the tropical sun, and for a long time he stroked the monkey's head. His fingers touched Lucy's, and hers didn't draw away.

"I paid 'im 'is bargain price. That, and a little more," said Mr. Mullock. "I 'eld out the money, and suddenly I saw that I knew 'im. I recognized that wreck of a face. Not a month before, this old man and I 'ad ridden to 'ounds together. Oh, 'e'd been young and 'andsome then; I couldn't believe the change. I withdrew my money, and 'e 'owled. Such a cry! Such misery."

"Was he mad?" asked Lucy.

"Not at all. Up 'e went and fetched the stone," said Mr. Mullock. "Thrust it at my 'and. 'Touch it,' said 'e. 'Just touch it once, I beg you.' And I did. It had a thousand facets,

Lucy Elizabeth, and in each one I saw a thing I wanted, or a thing I wished to be. Not five minutes later I left that place with—"

"The Jolly Stone," I finished for him.

Mr. Mullock looked more than surprised. "You know it?" he asked.

"Know it?" I said. "I *own* it, Mr. Mullock. I held it in my hand."

"Hah!" he said. *"Hah!"* he cried, sitting up. "Then it's over. I'm freed from the thing." A huge grin spread across his face, before quickly vanishing again. "But 'ow do I know it's really the Jolly Stone? Did you find it in the river, boy? In the Thames, near the Tower Stairs?"

"Yes," I said. It had been exactly there.

"When?" he asked. "What day did you find it?" Then, "No, I'll tell you!" he cried. "It was November last, was it not? No, wait! It must have been the day I was given the boat on Botany Bay. Hah! It was September when you pulled the stone from the river."

"Yes," I said, and he gloated. He was right; it had been September. But as surprised as I was, Lucy Beans was even more so. "Botany Bay?" she asked. "What were you doing there?"

"Fishing. Every morning I sailed out and jigged on the reefs. I was . . ." He sighed. "Well, I was a convict, missus. I still am; you might as well know it, and you can wash your 'ands of me now. I'm an escaped convict, just like the boys 'ere."

"You were transported?" said Lucy. "For what crime? Stealing diamonds, I suppose."

177

"Stealing bread," said Mr. Mullock. "I got seven years for a loaf of stale bread."

"A rich man stealing bread?" She sounded unbelieving.

"I wasn't rich for long," said he. "Not after the Jolly Stone came into my 'ands. Hah! 'Ow my fortunes took a tumble. From rags to riches, I'm back to rags before you say Jack Quick. Along with the stone came the curse, the ruination."

"But you threw it away," I said.

"Worst thing I could 'ave done." He drew in his legs and crossed them. He cuddled the monkey as if it were a baby. "The curse must pass from 'and to 'and. For your sake, boy, I 'ope you've put that stone where someone's going to pick it up."

"It lies six feet down in a London grave," I said. "But I'm not lost, Mr. Mullock. Not yet . . ."

"Hah! Who's going to find it there?" he asked. "No one in *your* lifetime."

"I'll dig it up myself," I said. "I only have to get home to do it."

"Only 'ome," he said, with unusual softness. "Only 'alf a world to travel, and misfortune every mile. You've a 'ard road ahead, Tom Tin."

"Yes, I believe that's true," I told him.

"Well," he said, turning to Lucy Beans. "Now you know what I am, do you 'ate me for it?"

"How can I hate a man for stealing bread?" she asked. "Or is there more? How did you escape?"

"I didn't hexactly escape at all," he said. "I went to the boat one morning, and found six men 'iding under the sail.

The most vicious men you've ever seen. They were going to be 'anged that morning, but they killed a priest and the guards, then told me to sail them to the islands. It put me on the run, but what was I to do? It was that or 'ave my throat cut, so out I went to the reefs, and through them and beyond. First island we came to, a month at sea, they set about murdering each other, Lucy Beans. All the time I believed I'd be next."

I watched Mr. Mullock closely. He seemed to be telling the truth. At least he spoke in a heartfelt way, and I could see that Lucy believed him. So did Boggis, I thought. There was no doubt how Midgely felt. He lowered his parasol, looked toward Mr. Mullock, and told him, "You'll inherit the earth; that's what Tom says. The meek, they always inherit the earth."

"Well, thank you, son," said Mr. Mullock, still gazing at Lucy. "There, you know mine, Lucy; what's *your* story?"

It was much longer than Mr. Mullock's, and not half as rummy. I lost interest while she was still a girl in finishing school, merely dreaming of travel someday. As she rambled through her life, I watched the distant sail gliding slowly along.

All day it was there. At dusk it was beating north, and at dawn it was beating south. I wanted it to vanish, so that we might get on our way and fetch, at last, the elephant island where my father waited. If waiting he was.

Mr. Mullock too looked every so often to see if the sail was there. The one time it wasn't—when the ship was passing behind an island—his face rather crumpled. I saw that, and knew why. He and Lucy were falling in love.

They smiled more readily, and laughed more easily. Hand in hand they walked the island, their joined arms swinging high and fast. I saw them coming over the rise in the middle, Mr. Mullock's hat and head and shoulders appearing, then Lucy beside him, with her head turned up. I felt a terrible jealousy—not that they were together, but that Midgely was with them. He trotted along beside Lucy, holding his white parasol. The ache in my heart was wicked, for I was certain that Midgely had never been happier.

"Is this what it's like to have a mum and a dad?" he asked me. Mr. Mullock was cutting wood for the steamboat. "Is it?"

"I suppose so," I told him.

"What do you mean?" he said. "You *know* what it's like; you've always had a mum and a dad."

I was twisted inside. It wasn't that I *envied* Midgely; truly, I was pleased for him. I didn't really know why it pained me to sit alone and see the three of them together.

For three days the sail was like a sentry that kept me prisoner. I decided that Mr. Mullock was right, and the curse of the Jolly Stone was what kept it patrolling back and forth in the one direction I had to go. On the third day it was there at twilight. Hours later, in the pitch black, the sky twinkled with cannon fire. We heard the shots in a faint thundering.

"They might be after the junglies," said Mr. Mullock. "They may be pounding a village." But all I could think was that—for some strange reason—they were shelling my father's ship.

On the following morning, the sail vanished. It slipped over the eastern horizon, and didn't reappear at all that day.

When it hadn't returned by noon of the next, I said, "It's time. We have to go."

Mr. Mullock sighed and grumbled. "Tom, look," he said. "Son, listen." He put his hand on my shoulder and led me away from the others. The monkey was riding on his shoulder, its tail round his neck like a fuzzy collar. When we'd gone a few yards he turned me round to face him. "I'll tell you straight out, Tom," he said. "We're not leaving this island."

twenty-two

WE SAY OUR FAREWELLS

Mr. Mullock wasn't angry. He didn't rant and rage as he'd done before. But I could see that he was deadly serious. "That's the way of it," he said. "We're not leaving 'ere."

"Not leaving?" I echoed. "Well, *I'm* going, Mr. Mullock. I'm going whether you like it or not."

He looked astounded. "You muggins," he said. "Of course you're going. It's me who's staying, you chump of wood. Me and Lucy Elizabeth."

"And Midgely?" I asked.

"Well, that's for Midgely to say." He was more caring than I would have thought possible. "The same goes for you, my boy, and that juggins too. All of you can stay if you like."

"You know I can't do that," I said.

"Well, know this too; you're safe 'ere," he told me. "That

182

ship 'as done its searching and won't search again. Out there you'll be 'unted. You'll be 'ounded."

"It doesn't matter," I said.

"It's you who's cursed now. You see that, don't you?"

"If that's so, then I'm not safe anywhere," I said.

"Better 'ere than there." He pointed to the east. "You'll only meet up with more of them, 'eadhunters, cannibals, and all sorts of gruesome beasts. You can't imagine the powers in the Jolly Stone."

If I had let him talk any longer, he would have kept me on the island. Perhaps that was the Stone at work; it was what the curse was meant to bring me. I squared my shoulders and told him, "I'm leaving. Alone or not, I'm leaving now."

"I thought as much," he said. "What you've started, you'll finish. I've seen that in you all along."

I wondered if he was trying to flatter me. Perseverance was not something I had ever seen within myself.

"Cursed or not, I can't go with you, lad," he said. "I can never go 'ome to England. You know the 'ardest thing to bear? That those who knew me will always think I'm a killer. And I'm hincluding you as well."

I didn't understand right away.

"You're not sure of it yourself," said Mr. Mullock. "After all that's 'appened, you're still not sure of it." He sighed. "Well, how could you be? You weren't in Botany Bay when the Gypsy chopped the priest. You weren't on my island to see the madness. You'll always wonder 'ow the Gypsy died. You can't even say what 'appened to Early."

He was right; I would never really know any of it.

"That's the curse, you see," he said. "It's why you took

the axe from me, and why you made me fear that every night could be my last. It means you'll never trust a soul. If they're not after the diamond, they're after you. I know that, lad; it did the same for me."

I had never once thought that Mr. Mullock had any fear of me. For the first time, though, I saw that what had happened between us might seem different through his eyes.

"I don't envy you, lad," he said. "But you're not lost. Not yet. I thought I was doomed to misery, but look at me now. Just days ago I was on a wretched island, in the company of killers, and 'ere I am in the Garden of Eden, with the prettiest woman in the world. What finer place could we choose than this to make a 'ome? Everything we want is 'ere."

"You don't want very much, then," I said.

"True enough," said he. "Only 'appiness and each other. Why, look, it won't be a family we'll be starting. It will be a people, won't it? A whole new world of Mullocks."

"And a happy one, I think." I meant it. No matter what he'd done or what he was, Mr. Mullock was a better man than he'd been when I met him.

We shook hands and I left the island that very hour. I had nothing to collect, no belongings to take. I walked down to the boat, and all came with me. Midgely, with his parasol, held hands with Lucy Beans. It didn't seem that he would leave the island. When I stepped into the steamboat, it pleased me that Boggis came right behind me. But it was Midgely I wanted, and at that moment I knew why my heart had been aching so badly. I had feared all along that this would happen.

"Tom," he said. "Tom, I can't see you."

Lucy led him to the water. She brought him down the bank, then left him with me. He looked quite old and worried. His hand rested on the gunwale. "I suppose they'll look after me here," he said.

"I'm sure they will," said I.

He nodded, then sniffed. "But, Tom? Oh, Tom, can't I go with you?"

"You want to?" I asked.

"More than anything, Tom," said he.

I laughed in delight. "Why didn't you tell me that?" I said.

"You never asked," he said. "I thought you was like my mum, that you was glad to see the back of me. Oh, Tom, I want to go where you go."

I helped him over the side and into the boat. Boggis had a fire burning already, and smoke was rising into the trees. We untied our lines. We pushed away from shore. Boggis worked the levers and the dials. The engine thumped and hissed, and the paddle wheels began to turn.

"Good-bye!" shouted Lucy. "Godspeed to you all."

Midgely was waving madly.

"Good luck!" cried Mr. Mullock. "Live large, you 'ear. Live large and die 'ard, Tom Tin."

I waved. For a moment I saw the two of them arm in arm, one dressed in white, the other in black, and then both were hidden by the trees. I turned away and didn't look back. None of us looked back, until the low island was out of sight.

But I couldn't get them out of my mind. I thought of Mr. Mullock and the curse of the Jolly Stone. I worried about what might await us at the elephant island. Then into my thoughts came the *chuckatee-chickadee* of the engine, and it reminded me of Lucy. I knew that Midgely was thinking of her. His face had a moony, faraway look; his hands caressed the parasol. Would it have been kinder if I'd made him stay behind?

None of us talked very much, and least of all him. We pushed along with the wind behind us, so that we chased our own smoke all through that long day.

At night we drifted. We doused the wood from the firebox and left it steaming in the bucket. Then we lay in the bottom of the boat, and the rain came down as the wind picked up. From the south, it blew hard. The waves piled; they rumbled and broke and hammered on the planks. I wrestled again with the seasickness, and with my old fear of the water. As the waves grew higher, as they slammed more heavily against the wood, I thought that we would soon be flooded, or smashed to splinters. But the boat weathered the blow, and when I lifted my head in the morning there was sunshine all around, sunshine and a big double rainbow that arched from the sea.

It was like a mysterious bridge, a phantom of shimmering colors. And right below the arch, framed in the streaks of red and blue and yellow, was Midgely's elephant island.

The shapes of the land, the pattern of rocks and trees, formed an enormous head. Gray cliffs gave it spreading ears and a trunk that curled back on itself. Veins of stone and running water formed a pair of curved tusks.

I stood up, the seasickness forgotten. "Midge," I said. "Midge, we've found it."

"The island?" he asked. He turned his dead eyes to the sea. "What does it look like, Tom?"

"Like an elephant." There was nothing more I could say. Its skin was rippled and wrinkled by the folds of land. There were even nubbins of rock for its eyes. "It looks exactly like an elephant, Midge."

"I know that, Tom," he said. "But what does an elephant look like?"

I couldn't help laughing. All this time we'd been searching for an island that Midgely wouldn't have recognized if he'd still had eyes that could see. "It doesn't matter," I said. "It's big and green and beautiful."

Boggis scratched his head. "I didn't know elephants were green."

We stoked the fire and steamed toward the island. We spewed more smoke than had ever come from the Limehouse chimneys, but that didn't matter to me. It was wonderful to be rushing toward the rainbow and the island in its middle. As I stood at the tiller, as the smoke swirled from the funnel and hid the colored bands in the sky, I recalled an old tale of my mother's. *"Never pass through a rainbow,"* she'd told me, one rainy afternoon. *"Pass through a rainbow, and you can't ever get back."*

It was an impossible feat, I thought. Rainbows had always moved away as quickly as I'd gone toward them. But this one seemed to hover where it was, and I had to look higher and higher to see its arch. When passing clouds darkened the sky, and at last the colors dissolved, I wondered if it was somehow still there above them, and if we didn't go steaming right through it.

Boggis stuffed the firebox until the metal glowed. The little valves chattered and whined, and bubbles of smoke burst blue and black into the air. I wondered if my father was watching it, if he could see the sunlight sparkle on the boat, and if he was even then turning a spyglass toward us.

I had to shout, almost, for Midgely to hear. "Where's the harbor? Which side of the island?"

"North and east," said Midgely.

I wondered if I should circle the island to get there, or land somewhere else and go on by foot. But after all my waiting, I couldn't wait another moment. I steered for the tip of land on the eastern side. It was below the point of the elephant's tusk, a jagged fringe of trees.

The island changed when we drew closer. As the rainbow had done, the elephant's head dissolved. Where its trunk had been was suddenly nothing but hills and rock. The ears became nothing more than stony cliffs, and I couldn't find where I'd once seen the tusks. It gave me a small shudder to think that we would have missed the island altogether if we'd come at it from a different side.

Boggis scurried for more wood. He pulled an armload from the stack beside the engine, then straightened up and seemed to turn to stone. He stood like that, unmoving, as the boat tipped on a wave and rose on another. The wood tumbled from his arm as he pointed ahead. He looked back, shouting something that I couldn't hear. And with a terrible thump the boat hit something hard.

I heard it bang on the bow, then bang again on the keel. It missed the paddle wheels, but thumped below me as we ran it over. I saw it surface behind us, breaching from the foam in our wake. A big slab of white wood, it stood up on its side and slowly fell flat.

It was the side of a boat, or part of one. The planks were shattered and torn.

Boggis ran to the engine, to the big levers and wheels. Down our left side passed a barrel, down our right a broken spar and a tangle of rope.

With a shrill blast, the engine blew off its steam. A white cloud shot out from the valves, with a shriek that nearly pierced my ears. The paddle wheels made a breathy, shuddery sound in the water. They no longer drove the boat, but slowed it, and we began to wallow in the waves.

"What's wrong?" asked Midgely.

More wreckage drifted by. I saw the white bow of a boat, then the stern. I thought I saw the head of a man, but it was only a wooden pulley.

"Tom, what's happened?" said Midgely.

"The sea's all full of bits," I said. "There's wood and rope and everything all floating around."

"I wonder what is it," he said.

I was afraid I knew already. By the look on Midgely's face, he must have thought the same. The cannon fire that we had seen in the night, only that could have caused this ruin. But what ship lay shattered around us?

We steamed on, more slowly. I watched barrels rolling in the waves, and chunks of wood so blown apart that I couldn't tell what was what. Boggis tried to catch something as it drifted by, just below the surface. I saw his hand dip in, then a shape appear as he pulled. It was a trouser leg that he held, and a man's foot that rose white from the sea. He dropped it, and it sank again in our wake.

I looked at the island, at the fringe of trees. A speck of

color there caught my eye, but it was several minutes before I could see what it was. I made out the two masts and spars of a brig, a topsail furled on its yard. Beyond those trees in the island's harbor, a vessel had come to rest. The speck of color was a flag, and in a moment that was both terrible and wonderful, I recognized its pattern. The Goodfellow flag. I was looking at the masts of my father's ship.

Where the wreckage had come from was a mystery. It was a mystery that I didn't care to solve just then, for my father was safe in the harbor, and I wanted only to reach him. I had Boggis stoke the fire again, and we plunged across the waves. He pointed to the left or right, and I steered past timbers, past staves and broken planks that tipped over the waves ahead and slipped away behind.

I rounded the point of land. I turned into the harbor. Straight ahead stood the masts of my father's brig. They were tall and straight, the yards neatly crossed.

But I felt little joy at the sight. For it was *only* the masts that I saw. They poked straight from the water itself, straight from the sea to the sky. My father's ship lay deep beneath the waves.

twenty-three

TOWARD THE ELEPHANT ISLAND

I steered across the bay, feeling that what I saw could not possibly be true. That if I kept going toward those masts the hull would appear below them. Surely it was only hidden by a strange mirage, a trick of the shoreline or a quirk in the clouds. It had to be so. It wasn't right—it wasn't fair—that I could come all this way for nothing.

As the steamboat shook and chugged along, I looked nowhere else but at those masts. Boggis did the same, and no one watched behind. We saw the rigging stretching down, the braces and the stays, the ratlines and the halyards, all leading into the sea. Some were broken, others tangled, but the yards were squared and the sails furled; the ship seemed to lie at anchor.

As we neared the masts, Boggis slowed the engine to a

heartbeat thump. We glided between the mizzen stays, and I looked down through the water at the hatches and deck. I saw the spoked wheel rippling as though it were turning. A gleam of light shone from a sword left lying at its base. We steamed slowly from stern to bow, staring down at a ship that had drowned.

I had always been selfish, but never more than then. My first thought was not for what had befallen my father, but for the terrible fix it had left me in. *Where am I to go from here, who is to help me now?* I wondered.

It was Midgely who tore me from those shameful thoughts. "Don't worry, Tom. They must have gotten ashore," he said. "They must be all right, don't you think?"

I couldn't imagine what had been said to make him realize the ship was gone. Perhaps he only sensed it, in that mysterious way he sometimes had. He was facing the shore now, with the handle of his parasol wedged by an elbow, his hands cupped to his blind eyes.

"Can you see the village?" he asked. "Can you see any sailors there?"

There were only trees ahead, and a brown river tunneling out from the jungle. I thought Midgely was wrong again, that the island was uninhabited, until I turned far enough to see the fringe of trees we had passed. There was his village, stretched along the shore, a long row of brown buildings standing on wooden stilts. On the beach below them was a line of canoes, and the Indians were already busily launching them.

"Lucky it's a friendly island," said Midge. "It's the friendliest of them all, you know."

I had steered between the masts and the rigging. We were passing then over the windlass, and I could see the bowsprit poking ahead through the water. One of the foresails had come loose, and it flapped in a current. A cloud of bright fish darted behind it and turned, all at once, to dash behind the bow.

"I wish Lucy Beans was here," said Midge. "She could talk to the Indians. She could ask what happened."

I steered between the forestays. I looked up along their length, to the tall mast that they braced, and saw the Goodfellow flag at the top. It fluttered on a sky full of ragged clouds, split by shafts of sunlight. I was looking at nearly the same sight I had seen day after day on our long voyage south, and in a flash of memory I recalled the moment when I'd found that my father was the captain. I felt the same joy and comfort, but not for more than a second.

Boggis cried sharply, "Tom, look!"

I thought he was shouting a warning that I was about to tangle the boat in the rigging. I pushed the tiller over, then saw him pointing back.

A rainbow stretched above the fringe of trees, one end on the shore and one on the water, as though we had, indeed, passed through it. At its watery end, something was moving in a haze of clouds. I couldn't quite see what it was, but I *heard* it then. Across the bay came the splash and thump of a hundred paddles.

"Is it them?" asked Midgely. "Is it the headhunters, Tom?"

Out from the rainbow, from its glow of colors, came a whole fleet of canoes. There were small ones and large ones, some driven by a single man, others by a dozen. They formed a line right across the bay, trapping us at its head.

"Tom, tell me!" cried Midge. "Is it the headhunters in that big canoe?"

"No. I don't know who it is," I said.

Boggis leapt to the wood; he stuffed the firebox. He pushed the lever, and the engine raced; the pistons whirled. "Break through them!" he cried. "It's our only hope."

I turned the tiller. I aimed the boat for the mouth of the bay, and the paddle wheels beat at the water.

"No!" shouted Midgely. His parasol tumbled into the bottom of the boat as he threw himself across the tiller. "What about your dad?" His voice slurred in excitement. "Don't you want to shee what happened to the shailorsh?"

"Never mind him, Tom. It's too late for them," said Boggis.

The steamboat was surging forward. Ahead lay the freedom and safety of open water. Once we'd charged through the canoes, there wasn't one that could catch us. It was go on and escape, or stay and . . . And what? And battle the savages? We were already too late. We could be of no help to my father.

Waves spread behind us. They rolled through the rigging of my father's ship. They splashed against the masts. High in the mizzen, a pulley swung on a broken halyard and rang against the mast like the tolling of a wooden bell. Boggis had the firebox open. He was throwing in the wood that Mr. Mullock had cut.

Our wake spread farther and faster. Spray tossed high at the bow. The canoes were closing together into a pack, like wolves on the water. I looked at my father's ship; back at the canoes.

"Full steam!" I said.

"Tom, no!" cried Midgely.

But I pushed him away, then turned the boat and aimed it, not at the canoes, but straight for the river.

Our smoke was thick and billowing. The fire raged in its box, and steam shot whining from the valves. We crossed our own wake, rolling far to the side as we battered through it in a cloud of spray. We passed between the masts of my father's ship, over the drowned hull, then up the bay with the trees flicking by on the shore.

The water turned from blue to brown as we met the currents of the river. They pushed the boat sideways; they nearly spun it around before I straightened us out again. The water boiled around the hull, streaming foam in streaks behind us, but the trees on the shore passed less quickly, and then less quickly still.

The canoes gained on us as we fought against the river. I watched the ripples and the eddies, and steered where the water was smooth. It brought us close to one bank, then right across to the other, and the branches of trees scraped on the engine, and the smoke tangled up in the leaves. I looked back again, and was afraid to look a third time.

But the river that slowed us slowed them as well. And the mechanical arms of the steam engine never tired. They went round and round, and back and forth, and pushed us up the river.

The river narrowed; the banks closed in. For a terrible minute it seemed that we weren't moving forward at all. Then slowly the shores spread apart, and the trees went by again. A crocodile, riding the current, hurtled past like a green torpedo.

Round a bend, round another, we beat our way into the heart of the island. The trees grew taller, and they reached their branches across the river. We surged through a tunnel that was surely too small for the red canoe. But we pushed on, turning left where another stream came in to meet ours, left again each time it divided. Then we heard a roar and rumble ahead.

Around the next bend we found a waterfall. It stretched from bank to bank, a rocky ledge where the river tumbled into tea-colored foam. It wasn't more than five feet high, but it might have been a Niagara. We couldn't go around it, and we couldn't go up it. Our journey had come to an end.

There was a broad pool below the falls, and a narrow, tepid stream flowing into it. I drove the boat full steam at its mouth, crashing through branches. They swept aside and closed behind us, and we ground to a stop in the midst of the jungle, wedged between the muddy banks like a cork in a bottle. Boggis stopped the engine. "Douse the fire," I said.

As he brought out the tongs and the bucket, I scrambled to the front of the boat. I could see nothing but leaves all around us. But when I leaned over the bow and pushed the ferns apart, I found a huge fallen tree lying across the stream. It was so close that I could nearly touch the bark. Had the water been a little higher, or our speed a little greater, we would have smashed ourselves right into that tree.

I was pleased to think how well hidden we were. When the fire was out, and the smoke stopped rising, the boat would never be found unless the savages blundered right up the stream. It was jammed so tightly in place that I saw no need to tie it to the trees.

We listened for canoes, but all I heard was the river spilling over the falls. Its steady rumble was loud enough to mask the approach of a dozen canoes, but every time I heard the splash of paddles, it turned out to be only the churning of the water.

"We can't just sit here," I said. "There's nothing gained by that."

"Then what do we do?" asked Boggis.

"We have to go to the village," I said. "Or at least *I* have to go."

But how? In the twists and branches of the river I had lost all sense of direction. I was afraid I would go into the jungle and never come out. And I was too scared of crocodiles, and even of the brown water itself, to go swimming and wading into the river. I wondered if we could wait for darkness and let the currents drift the steamboat down to the bay. But the thought of what might lurk on those banks was even more terrifying.

How many hours of daylight were left? Whatever I did, I wanted to have it finished by nightfall.

As I wrestled with the choices, a rain began falling. It beat on the trees and dripped on the boat, becoming increasingly heavy. In the heat of the jungle, it was more misery than relief. Midgely raised his parasol, and the drops clinked off the metal of the engine.

Then I heard a howling in the trees. It was an unearthly, terrible sound, not human at all, and with it came a loud rustle of branches and leaves.

"Holy jumping mother of Moses. What's that?" asked Midgely.

I found it easier to go and look, for it was a horror to sit where I was and only imagine. I went to the bow of the boat. I pushed aside the ferns again. I looked up. And there, moving across the jungle top, was a man all covered in orange hair. His arms and legs were unnaturally long, his face flat and brown. Another moved behind it, swinging from branch to branch. Then more appeared, all traveling through the world at the roof of the forest. Their hands were huge, with hairy backs and leathery palms, much like those of the little monkey that had befriended Mr. Mullock. But these creatures weren't quite monkeys, and they weren't quite men. They were part of each, wildmen of the jungle.

The rain became nearly solid. I had to shield my eyes and peer between my fingers. The first of the wildmen stopped, nearly right above me, and squatted on a thick branch. One of his hands reached out and broke off an enormous leaf. He held it above his head like an umbrella, and all the others—the whole tribe of wildmen—did the same. They settled in the crooks of branches, each with his own umbrella, and sat quiet and hunched, with looks of gloom on their strange faces.

One chattered, and another answered. Then, all together, they turned and looked down. And out from the jungle stepped a man—a savage in a loincloth. He was bent under a heavy weight.

twenty-four
"THEY'S ALL DEAD, AIN'T THEY?"

The savage carried one end of a pole. It rested on his shoulder as he stepped quickly from the trees and up to the log that lay right before me. I knew that if he glanced to the side he would see me. But he kept his head down, with the rain splattering on his hair, and I heard the padding sounds of his feet on the wood. I saw water ooze from the bark where his weight pressed down.

Trussed to the pole was a man with no head. I knew at once he'd been a sailor. He wore tarpaulin trousers and a sailor's jacket. He dangled from the pole with his legs and arms crossed above it.

A second savage carried the other end of the pole. A third bore the head by its hair. It swung from his hand, turning slowly left and slowly right. For a moment it seemed to stare at me. With open eyes, and a mouth showing white teeth, it wore a look of utter terror. I shivered from the shock of this, for I had known the man. It was Willy Bede, my father's steward.

The savages trotted on, over the log and into the jungle again, watched by the wildmen above. I drew back into the steamboat. Boggis gasped. "Why, you look like you seen a ghost," he said.

I was shaking from head to toe as I sat beside Midgely. The head of Willy Bede still swung before my mind's eye, all etched so clearly that I thought I would never forget the ragged flesh at its neck, and the man's awful look.

"What did you see?" asked Midgely.

He paled when I told him. So did the giant Boggis, who looked frightfully small just then. "We came too late," he said. "They's all dead, ain't they?"

"Don't say that," I told him. "I don't believe they're all dead, and I'm going to the village to look. That path must lead there."

"I want to go with you," said Midgely.

"Well, you can't," I told him. "I won't take you."

"Then Gaskin will," said Midge.

But Boggis shook his head. "I ain't going to the village, am I, Tom?"

"No, you don't have to," I said.

I was disappointed, though, until he nodded and said to Midge, "I'll be looking in them hills, you see. There might be others hiding in the hills."

We left Midgely sitting under his parasol, with a circle of water dripping all around him. Boggis and I climbed to the log, with the wildmen peering down upon us. They looked wise, somehow, as though wondering why men weren't as peaceful as beasts.

"We'll meet back here," I said to Boggis. "If I haven't returned by morning, you'll know that . . ." I couldn't say it. "You'll have to take the boat yourself. You and Midge. Will you see he's safe?"

He nodded. "I will, Tom."

I went at a run, and despite the rain I sweated in the jungle heat. My breaths burned in my throat and lungs. The path went nearly straight, uphill and down, and at every stream was a log for a bridge.

I ran a mile and walked a mile, afraid I'd overtake the savages. I passed through jungle and swamp, then down a long hill to the sea, all the time hearing the whistle of birds, the chirp of cicadas. When the path veered close to the shore, where it started out along the spit, I heard drumming begin in the village. Voices rose in shouts and shrieks. I jogged along the trail until I came to the first hut. Then I took to the jungle, creeping from tree to tree, and came to the clearing where the savages feasted.

The man who had carried Willy Bede's severed head was dancing with his trophy. Round and round he went, leaping, spinning, twirling in a flash of bones and feathers. A great crowd swarmed around him, and he danced through the middle of it. He held the swinging head high, then held it low, then whooped and shook the thing. He thrust it here, then thrust it there, then danced it round behind the drummers, down between the fires that crackled and raged at the center. Through the rain and smoke he spun with the head. Then the drums beat faster, and the crowd closed round him, and I saw the head rise up above them all, now speared on the end of a wooden stake.

With a shout and a cheer, the dance went on. Women clapped their hands and shook their hips; children ran shrieking through the crowd. Then the stake was mounted in a row of others, at the front of the largest hut. Four heads, with grisly grins, looked out above the village and its wild celebration. I recognized one as a helmsman I'd liked, another as the carpenter who had fixed the longboat what seemed like years before.

The crowd fell apart, and I saw a fire that had been knocked down to coals and embers. Turning above it was the body of poor Willy Bede, still trussed to the stick like a pig. At either end was a savage to turn it, and that ghastly thing flopped over and over again.

I turned away, sickened and scared. So even my father hadn't known of all the dangers. Or he hadn't told us that there were headhunters who were cannibals too. I slipped silently into the jungle, and didn't emerge again till dusk.

The celebration was still going on. I judged by the heaps of charcoal, and by the pile of long bones, that it was already many days old. Strangely, I found hope in that, for I imagined it would never stop as long as a sailor was alive on the island.

The trussed body still hung from its stick, and every savage from the village seemed to be gathered round the fires. Most were seated on mats, though half a dozen worked at a pile of broad leaves, in a cloud of steam or smoke that swirled from the fronds. They poked long sticks right through them, into a hole dug underneath, a pit that I guessed was an oven cooking the remains of another slaughtered sailor.

I crawled from the trees, then dashed to the nearest hut, slipping into the darkness among its stilts.

It was a poor hiding place. The boards above me creaked as someone walked across the floor. I stole through the shadows to the next hut, threaded round the pilings, then crossed to the third, the largest of any.

Near its back was a hole in the floor, a pool of dim light. On the ground lay ashes and chunks of burnt wood, as though sweepings from a fire had been dropped down the hole. I moved toward it. I stood on the ashes, and peered up.

I heard the buzz of flies.

My mind recoiled at that sound. I remembered the trapper's hut, and the gruesome find I had made there. Here the sound of flies was tenfold louder, such a steady drone that the whole hut might have been a hive of giant bees. There were so many flies that it was the swirl of their black bodies that made the light flicker in the hole. I saw the glint of their wings, a fire-colored cloud swirling above me.

I shinnied up one of the stilts, then held on with my knees as I reached for the lip of the hole. I got one hand on it, then the other, and pulled myself through.

With one look inside, I wished I'd stayed on the ground. From end to end, the hut was hung with human bones. Old white skulls sat on posts, on shelves and rafters. From every corner they stared back with their blank-eyed bony faces. And in a cluster, like coconuts, swayed six or seven fresh heads.

I stood up in the hut.

The flies covered the heads so completely that I couldn't see the faces. But one I didn't need to see. It was smaller than the others, and the hair was bright orange. So Carrots had been caught. Surely Weedle and Benjamin Penny had been as well. I held out my hand to chase the swarm of flies away. They came off like a thick, black skin, and the faces underneath were not whole.

More gruesome a sight I couldn't fathom. I didn't know whose heads hung there, only that none was my father's, nor Weedle's or Penny's.

I dropped back through the hole. I brushed flies from my hair, from my clothes and my feet. I ran from there—to the next hut, and the next, right down the long row until I came to the end. Then, as I slipped below the very last hut, the clearing burst into light. The fires had been fed and stirred, and now they raged in tall towers of flames. They lit the jungle all around.

In the clearing was a row of small cages. They were not more than three feet high, not even that in width, but inside each was squeezed a man. At every cage was a face, and white hands clutching the bars. In the nearest was the fiddler from my father's ship. His bush of dark hair could not be mistaken.

In another cage were two faces. I saw Walter Weedle and Benjamin Penny locked together in a space not as big as a wardrobe. With each surge and crackle from the fires, another face caught the light. I recognized some but not others, and then I saw my father.

He huddled in his cage just as the wildmen had perched

in the trees, with his legs drawn up and his hands reaching up through the roof. I couldn't sort out the thoughts that passed through my mind. There was certainly a pleasure just in seeing him again, but a horror too, and a hopeless dread that I was powerless to help him. What were the cannibals planning for these men?

I didn't have to wait to find out. Across the clearing, a savage approached. His face was painted, his arms tattooed. He wore shells and bones that clicked and rattled as he walked. He went straight to the first cage and opened a latch. The door was far smaller than the cage. He pulled it open, reached inside, and hauled out the fiddler.

Back toward the fires, the cannibal hauled the man along. He pushed him up against a stake at the center of the clearing, and others bound the fiddler to it by his hands.

The drumming had been slow and steady, but now it quickened. Warriors in their breastplates, with their shields and knives and feathered caps, began to circle the man at the stake. They passed behind him and before him, brandishing their spears. Round they went in a tightening circle. Then, one by one, they struck the man, whirled away, and—whooping—circled round again.

I couldn't see the fiddler through the rush of bodies, and I was glad for that. I saw the firelight splash on the knives of the savages, on their legs and their arms, and I heard the awful screams of the fiddler. All the while, the women danced and the children laughed, and the drums beat on.

The rain fell harder. It pounded on the huts and pounded on the clearing. It pounded on the sea with that sound that was like a running river. But the fires never faltered, and the savages never stopped. At last the fiddler fell quiet, and I saw him—as the circle of dancers widened—slumped at the stake with his head hanging down. Then the drums beat faster than ever. There was one more flash of a knife, one more shriek, and the fiddler's head rolled away across the ground.

The tattooed savage went back to the cages. He hauled out the next sailor, who dropped to his knees and begged for mercy, his hands held up as though in prayer. I knew him then; it was the fellow who had dressed as Neptune when we'd crossed the equator. I remembered how he'd roared with laughter that day, and I looked aside now as he sprawled on the ground, screaming for help. I heard him struggle and kick as he was dragged along. Then the dancing and drumming began anew.

If I waited any longer, my father would be next at the stake. But what could I do? How could I stop it? To reach the cages, I would have to cross the clearing. Even if I circled round behind the village, I would have to cross a broad part of it on the other side. I couldn't get past the savages, so I somehow had to get the savages away. But one boy against a tribe of cannibals: was there any hope at all? I wondered if I had time to look for Boggis and Midgely, and if it would really help to have them. What could the three of us do that I couldn't do alone?

I drew back in the darkness below the hut. I crawled down its length and out to the beach, not with any scheme in mind, but only to spare myself from seeing the warriors dance with their glittering knives. I wished I could escape the sounds as well—the drumming and shouts, and the screams of the man—but they followed me then, and would follow me always.

On the beach, the rain was falling hard. It carved rivers and ruts in the sand; it dashed on the water with a humming, hissing din. I spread my arms, looked up, and let it fall on my face, and I wondered and wondered: *how can a boy beat a village?*

Through my mind passed stories I had half forgotten, little bits from dreary hours of history classes. I tried to remember how tiny forces had beaten great armies, and I thought of the Trojan horse and the Minutemen at Lexington, of Sir Francis Drake and the Spanish Armada, Bonnie Prince Charlie and Rogers' Rangers, but not of a single time when a boy had beaten a village.

My head spun with the tales as I walked along the dark beach. I passed the next hut, into the glow of the fires, and saw the cannibals leaping past the flames. The light shone out into the bay, and I imagined that something out there was moving across the water. From the corner of my eye, for an instant I saw it. Was it the curve of a ship's bow? The loom of a sail? I peered into the darkness, and . . . there! Didn't I see a flicker of light, as faint as a match being struck?

A moment later my joy was followed by a crushing disappointment. There *was* a ship out there, and I had known it all along. My father's sunken ship, with its masts above the water, must have sat just where I was looking.

It seemed my last hope dissolved. I felt as beaten as I had in the old mission, when the cannibals had come with their torches. Then, from disappointment, I leapt to joy again. The fire that destroyed the mission had saved us. Might it save us again?

I made my way back to the largest of the huts. I ran as fast as a fellow could run on sand that caved at his feet. The drumming and the falling of the rain played fancies with my thoughts. I imagined I heard the gurgle of water at the bow of a ship, and the crack of a sail flopping over.

As I neared the hut, I saw someone plodding up the beach toward me, on a weaving course beside the water. I thought he wore a huge, domed cap. Then the firelight gleamed, and I saw that it was Midgely with his parasol, following the edge between the sea and the sand, guided by the firelight.

I had to pass the hut to reach him. He heard me coming and turned to dash toward the trees.

"Midge, wait!" I cried, as loudly as I dared.

"Tom?" he said.

I pulled him into the shelter of the trees. I wrenched the parasol from his hands and folded it shut. "I told you to stay with the boat," I said.

"I did, Tom. I did. But the rain flooded the river and carried the boat away."

I cursed myself for not thinking that would happen. "Is it gone?" I said.

"No, it ain't *gone*," said Midge. "We rode it down the river, me and Boggis. We rode it right to the sea, Tom, and then we tied it up. Gaskin's gone back to wait for you at the bridge."

I led him to the hut, to the heap of ash below the fire.

208

In the clearing, the drumming stopped, and a tremendous shouting and babble began. In only minutes, I thought, another man—perhaps my father—would be dragged from a cage.

I climbed through the hole. Midgely reached up with his parasol, and I pulled him after me. He swatted at the flies. He said, "Tom, we ain't alone in here."

I thought he saw, or somehow felt, the dangling heads above us.

But a hand came down on my shoulder. It turned me round, and I looked into the tattooed face of a savage.

twenty-five

AT A CANNIBAL FEAST

Midge and I were hauled down the length of the hut and pitched through its door. I tumbled onto the ground, and Midgely fell on top of me with his parasol.

The shouting of the cannibals rose higher as we sprawled into the firelight. Then it swelled to a fever as out from the jungle came six savages pulling Gaskin Boggis like a frightened horse. He fought and kicked, but they battered him down and stuffed him in a cage.

My father saw me and rattled at his bars. "Tom!" he shouted. "You filthy savages, keep your hands off my son!"

Midgely and I were crammed together into the last of the cages. Midgely still held the parasol that Lucy Beans had made him. He didn't shout; he didn't cry. He made no sound as the door was closed and a latch put on. The cannibals drew back to the fire.

My father kept shouting my name. His hand groped through the bars. "Oh, dear Tom," he said. "I prayed to see you one more time. I begged for that. God help me, I never thought it would come to this."

I still had one more hope, though it seemed nearly futile. The cannibals were dancing, the drums beating into that quick frenzy that had brought the end for the fiddler. I grabbed the parasol from Midgely's hands. I ripped the cloth apart, and the wires sprang loose. "Midge," I said. "Do you remember what you told me once? About killing dogs?"

Buffing, Midge had called it, long ago, when he'd told me of his crimes. *"You sell their skins,"* he'd said, and I suddenly smelled the stench of our prison ship; I saw him in its fetid darkness. *"You stick a wire in them. It goes right to their heart and does them in as gentle as you please."*

I grabbed a wire and tried to wrench it from the parasol. "Midge," I said. "Would it work on a man? Could you kill a man like that?"

"Golly, Tom," he said. "I don't think so."

The wire wouldn't come loose from the hub. I wrapped my fist around it as the cannibals suddenly whooped and cheered. I didn't look toward the fires.

"Why not?" I asked. "If it could kill a dog, why not a man?"

"Oh, it *could*," he said. "But, Tom, I can't do it. I can't see."

The wire heated in my fist as it bent and twisted. "Then show me," I said. "I'll do it."

Midgely's small hands felt across my shirt, then his finger poked at my ribs. "There. That's where you stick it, Tom. That's where."

The wire snapped. It sprang from my hand and flew against the cage. I thought it passed right between the bars, but with a tiny tick it bounced from the wood and fell across my leg. I took it up and held it tightly.

"Push hard," said Midge. "Push harder than you ever pushed."

Here came the savage, striding from the fires with his forked stick and its noose. I imagined myself jabbing the wire at his chest, driving it through his ribs. A cold sweat broke out on my back and my face and my hands. I said, "I can't. Oh, Midge, I . . ."

"You can," he said. "In your heart ain't you really the Smasher?"

"That was never me," I said. But was it really true? I had been born a twin, and I shared the cruel blood of my murderous brother. It had pulsed me into rages before.

"Just do it, Tom," said Midge.

The savage tugged at his noose. If he kept to his order, he would take my father next, then Weedle and Penny and all the others. Midge and I would be last, with no one to save but ourselves.

I shook the cage. "Take *me*!" I shouted.

"No!" cried Father.

But I shouted again, "Take *me*!" The savage came right to the cage as I cried out with every curse and oath I'd ever heard. Then he turned, and stepped toward my father.

I picked up the parasol and rattled at the bars. I worked it in between them and, clumsily, threw it at the man. He turned again. He came back to the door of my cage, bent down, and worked the latch.

His nose was pierced by a white bone. His earlobes had been slit and stretched, so that they dangled now—grotesquely—nearly to his shoulders. His dark tattoos were like patterns of little black rivets set into his skin. His hands were huge, and they fumbled with the latch.

I held the wire in my fists. I flexed it back and forth. My heart was pounding, but not with anger and rage. I felt nothing more than a sickening fear as the latch opened. The savage wrenched the door aside. He picked up his forked stick and thrust it into the cage.

I grabbed it. I pulled hard, and the savage toppled forward. His chest banged against the cage, and the strings of bones and shells swayed across the doorway.

I brought up the wire. I saw just where to aim it, just where to drive it in. But even then I knew I could never do it. I was not my twin after all; I had none of his cold fury. When my father had cut us apart, in the minute of my birth, he had made me very different.

The cannibal hauled me out and threw me to the ground. Before I could move, the noose encircled my neck.

"Tom!" my father shouted. "Oh, my dear son!"

The noose drew tight at my neck. I tried to work my fingers underneath the cord, but it was all I could do to keep my balance as the savage hauled me from the ground and marched me to the stake.

twenty-six

THE THIRD DANGER

I saw the crowd of cannibals turn toward me. A path opened between them, leading right to the stake. The warriors stood with their knives and spears. The drummers sat drumming, and the women danced. The children laughed and shouted.

The savage pushed me ahead. Around my neck, the noose drew so tight that I could scarcely breathe. I stumbled forward and the fires raged, sparks soaring high.

I could see a pool of blood around the stake, streaks along the wood. The savage turned me round.

As my back slammed against the stake, I heard a roar of sound, a whistle, and a crashing in the jungle. It all came nearly at once, and I didn't know what was happening. There was another boom, another shriek and crash.

"Cannons!" my father shouted. "Those are navy guns; six pounders. They're shelling the village."

So I *had* a seen a ship out there. Now, through the rain and darkness, came flares of light as the cannons fired. The balls smashed through huts, through trees and bushes.

The women fled. The warriors ran toward the beach. The children raced in both directions, and the clearing was suddenly empty. But the savage who held me didn't let go. With a shove on his stick he drove me to the ground, pinning me in its forked end. He put all his weight on it, pressing my face down in the red mud. I heard the cannonballs whistle. And suddenly the man was gone, and his stick thumped to the ground at my side.

From the beach came sounds of a battle—yells and screams, gunshots, and the clash of wood and metal. Of the savage there was no sign. He had simply disappeared.

I ran to the cages. I had to struggle at first with the latches, but each opened more quickly than the last. Out came the sailors, who fled from the clearing and vanished in the jungle's darkness. Out came Weedle and Penny, out came my father. But poor blind Midgely cowered in the cage. When I reached in, he screamed.

I said, "Midge, it's me."

My father and others were trying to free Gaskin. He wasn't moving. They pulled at his arms. "Come on!" they told him.

I hurried to help. But Gaskin had been beaten so badly,

215

so crammed in the small box that I feared his bones might have been broken. "It ain't no use," he said. "I can't move my legs. I can't even feel them, Tom."

"Leave him!" shouted Weedle. But Benjamin Penny had an even crueler mind. "Kill him, Weedle," said he, with a mad look. "Throttle him quick, and have done with it."

I refused to abandon Boggis. If I couldn't drag him out, I'd destroy the cage itself. So I went at it with fists and feet, flailing away at the wooden bars. My father attacked them too, and I heard them crack and splinter. A wall came away. The roof collapsed.

"Here they come again," said Weedle.

I turned and saw the cannibals swarming up from the beach. But now they ran all helter-skelter, scattering through the clearing. Behind them came a crowd of men more wild than any. In clothes of red and yellow, with long knives that flashed like streaks of flame, they might have sprung right out from the fires.

"Pirates!" shouted Father. "It's not the navy at all. God help us, it's pirates, Tom."

Together we got Boggis to his feet. But as soon as the giant tried to move, his legs buckled and he collapsed again.

"Oh, Tom," said Father. He put his arms around me for the first time since we'd been together on the ship. "We might as well stay with him and see the end right here. There's nowhere to go at any rate."

"But, Captain Tin," said Midgely. "We've got a steamboat on the beach."

My father made a grunting sound that might have been a

216

laugh. "A steamboat?" he said. "Why, you're a wonder, the pair of you."

We held Boggis between us, his arms resting on our shoulders. We staggered past the huts and down to the beach, then along the soft sand.

"You go ahead," said Father. "Get your fire stoked, your steam up. I won't come without the boy; don't worry."

Weedle and Penny needed no urging. They ran on into the rain and dark, that horrible Penny shuffling over the sand. But I stayed to help.

"Please go, Tom," said Father, puffing loudly now. "I beg you; do as I say."

The huts along the beach burst into fire one by one. The pirates were taking torches to them, and the flames leapt high and hot and bright. There was a clamor of high-pitched voices, and a score of pirates—maybe more—came along the beach behind us.

"Tom, go!" said Father, and I saw that he was right. I could help best by having the boat ready for him. So I led Midgely by the hand, as fast as we could move along the beach.

We found Benjamin Penny working at the knots that tied the boat to a tree. He was pulling and biting the rope. Weedle had known enough—or guessed enough—to open the fire-box and was filling it now with wood. They toiled in such a frenzy that I had no doubt they would have left without us.

Penny was cursing most foully. "It's all a tangle. A terrible quiz," he said.

"Pull on the end, you stupid," said Midgely. He elbowed

Weedle aside, found the tail end of the rope, and gave it a tug. The whole long knot unraveled. "You see? It's a chain knot. Now haul it in," he said.

Midge and I climbed into the boat. I dug out the matches and the oil can, and squirted the wood in the firebox. But it was too wet to catch a flame, and my matches fizzled one by one. The rain came down in torrents.

"Midge, where's that caul?" I said.

"It only works for drowning, Tom," he told me. "It don't save a man from pirates."

"We'll see about that," I said.

He fetched the box from its place and shoved it in my hands. I looked back and saw my father and Boggis staggering down the beach. The pirates seemed right at their heels.

"Hurry, Penny!" shouted Weedle.

I opened the wooden box. I sprayed oil inside it, all over the shriveled skin. I struck a match, then touched it to the oil, and flames leapt up in a greasy smoke. The old box—tinder dry—nearly exploded into fire. I shoved it on top of Weedle's wood, and slammed the door of the firebox.

There wasn't time to build pressure in the boiler. I pulled out the sculling oar and rammed it in its socket.

"Help me push!" cried Benjamin Penny. He had his bent shoulder pressed against the boat's bow.

"Wait!" I told him.

"Wal-ker!" said Weedle. "We ain't waiting for nothing." He jumped out to help Penny.

My father came wading through the water. All the light of the fires glowed on the surface, so that he seemed to be waist-deep in flames. He helped Boggis into the boat. He told Penny to get aboard, and even made a ladder of his hands to help him. The pirates were splashing through the sea, their swords and jewelry all aglow.

My father put his hands on the gunwale. But he made no effort to haul himself into the boat. He *pushed* instead. Though breathless and nearly done, he put all of his last strength into helping us escape.

"No!" I shouted. I tried to clutch his hands, but they moved away along the gunwale as the boat went sliding back.

"Do what's right by me, Tom," he said. "Do the handsome thing, my boy."

He pushed hard, and the effort unbalanced him. Facefirst, he fell in the water, and he was half drowned when he rose. But once more he lunged at the boat. His weight sent it moving faster.

"No!" I cried again. "Oh, Father, please, I need you!"

Everyone was shouting—the boys in the boat, and the pirates rushing. It was a mad babble of voices, but through it came my father's steady tones. He alone seemed sure and confident.

"You're all brandy, Tom," he said. "You're square aloft and trim below."

Benjamin Penny laughed. "Seasick at Chatham, that's your son. Seasick in a river, he was." The firelight glowed on his horrid face, and he grinned at me while the pirates fell upon my father.

They grabbed his arms, his shoulders, and his hair. Four

of them held him, and the others waded out toward the boat. But my father somehow struggled free. He shook off the men; he pulled away. And in the moment before they were on him again, he gave the passing bow a mighty shove that drove us clear.

"Godspeed, Tom," he said. "You've done me proud, my son."

"Proud?" shrieked Penny. "Why, he said he hated his father, that's what he said. Couldn't wait for the day—"

"You shut up!" I knocked him down, and he cackled his wicked laugh even as he crumpled. I couldn't believe he'd say such a thing. There was no rhyme nor reason to it. And his words may have been the last my father ever heard, for I saw a sword lifted high, a fabulous sword that glinted with a hundred jewels. It made a streak of light across the sky, and it felled my father in the water.

It was the hardest thing I'd ever done to turn the boat and scull it from the beach. I could see my father being hauled from the sea with his heels dragging in the sand. I knew there wasn't a hope in the world I could save him. But as I pushed the boat into the rain, as he faded away behind, I felt as though I'd betrayed my father.

"There ain't no one as brave as Redman Tin," said Midgely. "Ain't that true, Tom?"

"It is," I said.

Midgely nodded. "At least you know he won't be killed. Them pirates would never kill a man like him. They'll sell him for a king's ransom, won't they, Tom?"

"He'd rather be a dead man," I said. "He told us so himself."

"But if anyone can get away, it's Redman Tin," said Midge.

A whistle came from the steam engine as the pressure built up. I put away the oar and worked the wheel and levers. With a shudder, the paddle wheels turned. The pistons moved, the cranks went round, and I heard the sound that always made me think of a little girl, that *chuckatee-chickadee* of the engine working.

We moved faster. I steered to keep the burning village behind us, and we steamed through the rain. The black ship appeared ahead, a monstrous thing with many masts and great soaring cabins on the stern. It was the biggest ship I'd ever seen, so black and evil that I took one glance and turned away. I steered for the open sea.

Benjamin Penny was scuttling away toward Weedle, who had opened the firebox to put in more wood. The flames lit that horrid boy, glowing in the webs between his fingers. I despised him more than ever, and moved to hurry him on with a kick.

But there was a sudden flash, a roar and shriek, and the sea exploded into spray beside us. Weedle screamed. "What was that?"

"A cannon!" I shouted at him to close the firebox. "They're aiming for the light!"

He slammed the door. I hauled on the tiller. Another ball went shrieking past, and others followed. But the rest fell farther and farther astern, and soon the boat rose on the swells as we left the island behind us.

I sent Midgely to sit with Boggis. "How is he?" I asked.

It was Boggis himself who answered. "I'm better now, Tom," he said. "I'll start tending the fire in a minute."

"No, you rest," I told him. "Weedle and Penny will do that."

"Wal-ker!" said Weedle. "Why should we be the ones to work?"

"Because if you don't we'll strand you on the next island," I said.

He cursed. "Here, look, I didn't know you were the captain's boy. It's true, ain't it; you were never the Smasher?"

"No, he ain't old Smashy," said Benjamin Penny.

Weedle ignored him. "Tom, listen. It weren't my idea to take the boat and leave you. Mr. Mullock, he thought of that. 'Leave 'em behind,' he said. Well, where is he now, the old grub?"

"We left him behind," said Midgely.

Weedle grunted. "That's justice, ain't it?"

"No, it ain't, 'cause he ain't alone, is he?" said Midge. "We left him with Lucy Beans, but you don't know her, and more's the pity for you. She's a peach, ain't she, Tom? She's a plum, that Lucy Beans."

"By now he's bleeding all over from henpecks," said Weedle. "They'll be living the cat and dog life, him and the old bloss."

"She ain't an old bloss," said Midge. "Tell him, Tom. Tell him about Lucy Beans."

I didn't answer. I sat at the tiller, steering east into darkness and rain. The others squabbled and fought. "I'll give you a grueller," threatened Penny, and it seemed suddenly that little had changed since our first day together. We were fewer in number, and our boat was bigger and better, but we were still half a world from home, and no closer than when we'd started.

I shifted on the seat and made myself comfortable. I steered by the feel of the waves, listening to the *chuckatee-chickadee* of the engine. I sat and thought of my father.

"Do the handsome thing," he had told me. But what had he meant by that? *"Do what's right by me, Tom."*

He had left me with a riddle. One that I wasn't sure I'd ever solve.

epilogue

The rain stopped in the morning, and the sun beat down. Midgely wished for his parasol, as though it were the finest thing he had ever owned. His face was as red as a strawberry, and brown welts were forming on his lips. The tropics, I thought, were rotting him away, and I feared to look toward the shining boiler of the steam engine, lest I see the same tortured face reflected in the metal.

No one argued again over who would command the boat. I believed that Weedle thought I had a right to it, as the son of a captain. But Benjamin Penny seemed only to accept that he was powerless to change things. Or else he was waiting for just the right time to change them.

Not he, nor Weedle, nor even Boggis had any desire to go home to England. For now, they rode along on the same river of fate. There were many miles, and many days before us for that river to twist and turn.

We made only one more stop in the cannibal islands. I chose a place so small and flat that we could see right across it, from one end to the other. We reached it through a ring of reefs, and the steamboat sat in a stillness while the sea burst and broke all around.

Over the course of four days, we felled every tree on the island. We collected every coconut, every mollusk and every turtle that crawled on the beach. We left that island nearly as barren as the lonely rock where we'd found Mr. Mullock.

Every scrap of food we stored in the boat, along with as much wood as we could fit. The rest of the fallen trees we manhandled down to the water. We lashed them together into an enormous raft, and towed them astern as we passed through the reefs. I judged that we had enough fuel to last for at least a week, perhaps two. But our boat was so heavy, so dragged by the logs, that our speed was slowed to a crawl.

South and west we went, with the engine going *chickadee-chuckatee*. I hoped to pass south of all the islands and steam west to the Cape of Good Hope. Surely, I thought, we would find a ship that would take us home.

author's note

Britain sent its first lot of convicts off to Australia in 1787. In one stroke, conditions were improved in overcrowded prisons, and labor was provided to build a new British colony in the land "beyond the seas."

This wasn't a new idea. Britain had begun transporting convicts to North America more than a hundred and fifty years earlier. English criminals picked tobacco in Virginia, and grew sugarcanes in Jamaica. They helped establish colonies in Barbados and Canada and Singapore.

The "First Fleet" to Australia was made up of eleven ships. Provisioned by the government, and cared for by the navy, the convoy carried about 800 convicts, and everything that was needed to establish a new colony. It was an eight-month voyage to Australia, but every ship of the First

Fleet arrived safely, and fewer than thirty convicts died at sea.

Two years later, encouraged by the result, Britain prepared for the "Second Fleet," increasing the number of convicts to 1,006. But this time the government went about it in a different way. Instead of chartering the ships, they let out a contract to a private company.

The company was in the business of carrying slaves. So it packed the thousand convicts into just three ships, and spent as little as possible on food and supplies. This time the sea voyage killed more than one convict out of every four. Another 150 perished soon after reaching Australia. The transport *Neptune* left Britain with 499 convicts, but only 72 arrived in good health.

The Second Fleet was a terrible beginning to a new system of transportation. But with its navy needed for wartime duties, the government continued contracting ships to transport its criminals. So it examined the failings of the Second Fleet and laid down guidelines that improved conditions for the convicts. But there were still cruel captains and penny-pinching contractors. In 1796, six convicts were flogged to death with the cat-o'-nine-tails on the transport *Britannia*. In 1798, one third of the convicts aboard the *Hillsborough* died of starvation and typhus.

As the years went by, the system improved. By the time of Tom Tin, in the 1820s, a convict had a better chance of surviving his time at sea than did an ordinary seaman.

Altogether, until transportation ended in 1868, there was very nearly one shipload of convicts sent to Australia for every prisoner in the First Fleet. In those hundreds of ships in that century of voyages, there was only one successful mutiny. Escape attempts began with the First Fleet, when a convict rowed away from his ship during a stop in the Canary Islands. There is a doubtful story about another convict who is said to have hidden in his ship at sea, intending to emerge secretly in Australia and pass himself off as a free settler. According to the tale, he was deemed to have drowned, and was only discovered when he began pilfering from the captain's supply of champagne.

But many convicts escaped from their penal colonies in Australia. Uneducated, and with little understanding of geography, some thought they could flee overland to China. Some, like Mr. Mullock, took to the sea. One of the most famous escapes involved a woman.

Mary Bryant, of Cornwall, was sentenced to seven years' transportation for the crime of "highway robbery" after she and two other women robbed a lady of a twelve-penny silk bonnet and other small things. Bryant was shipped out in the First Fleet, on the transport *Charlotte*. It was a long voyage; she arrived in Australia with a newborn baby—named Charlotte, in honor of the ship.

In the penal colony of Botany Bay, Bryant married a male convict. He had been a fisherman in England, and now tended the nets that caught fish for Botany Bay. With him, Mary had another baby—a boy. In 1791, the whole family, and seven other male convicts, escaped in a six-oared cutter belonging to the colony's governor. Bryant's husband had secretly fitted the boat with supplies from a Dutch trader, including a compass and chart, food, and firearms.

The crew of convicts and children voyaged north up the

coast of Australia, and on to Timor, where Captain Bligh had landed after the mutiny on his ship, the *Bounty*. It was a distance of more than 3,000 miles for Mary Bryant and the others, and their voyage stood in comparison to Captain Bligh's for its hazards and unlikely success. They butchered turtles and made jerky from the meat. They used turtle fat to plug the leaks in the cutter's planks. They were chased, for part of the way, by cannibals in canoes.

At Timor, the convicts claimed to be survivors of a shipwreck. But they were eventually found out, and were arrested by a British captain who was hunting for the mutineers of the *Bounty*. He put them in irons and shipped them to the Cape of Good Hope. Mary's husband and son died on the way. Her daughter died during the voyage from there to England.

Mary Bryant was returned to prison as an escaped convict. She would have been transported for a second time if public sympathy hadn't saved her. Among her champions was the writer James Boswell.

Bryant became famous as the Girl from Botany Bay. She was pardoned for her crimes, and set free in Cornwall again.

acknowledgments

I would like to thank the many librarians who provided research material for this book, and especially Kathleen Larkin of the Prince Rupert Library. They unearthed old and obscure books that I could never have found on my own.

Thanks as well to my agent, Danielle Egan-Miller; my editor, Françoise Bui; and my partner, Kristin, who has probably read this story more times than I've read it myself.

about the author

Iain Lawrence studied journalism in Vancouver, British Columbia, and worked for small newspapers in the northern part of the province. He settled on the coast, living first in the port city of Prince Rupert and now on the Gulf Islands. His previous novels include the High Seas Trilogy: *The Wreckers, The Smugglers,* and *The Buccaneers;* as well as *Lord of the Nutcracker Men, Ghost Boy, The Lightkeeper's Daughter,* and *The Convicts,* the companion to *The Cannibals.*

You can find out more about Iain Lawrence at www.iainlawrence.com.